W9-BRO-991

CYBERIA

PRIME EVIL

CHRIS LYNCH

CYBERIA

PRIME EVIL

SCHOLASTIC PRESS
NEW YORK

All rights reserved. Published by Scholastic Press, an imprint of Scholastic Inc., *Publishers since 1920*. SCHOLASTIC, SCHOLASTIC PRESS, and associated logos are trademarks and/or registered trademarks of Scholastic Inc.

No part of this publication may be reproduced, stored in a retrieval system, or transmitted in any form or by any means, electronic, mechanical, photocopying, recording, or otherwise, without written permission of the publisher. For information regarding permission, write to Scholastic Inc., Attention: Permissions Department, 557 Broadway, New York, NY 10012.

Library of Congress Cataloging-in-Publication Data
Available

ISBN 978-0-545-02795-3

10 9 8 7 6 5 4 3 2 1   10 11 12 13 14

Printed in the U.S.A.   23
First edition, November 2010

The text type was set in Adobe Caslon.

To my sister, Dolly

I still can't believe she
went out with Dr. Gristle.

"Bucky?"

"Yes."

"Bucky Gristle? I am being sent away to be kept under the authority of somebody with the name Bucky Gristle?"

"Yes. What's wrong with that dog? Is he having some kind of convulsion?"

My dog, Hugo, is absolutely splitting his seams over my predicament. He is laughing so hard he may in fact swallow his tongue, but since I am the only one who can decipher him, this looks to everyone else like some kind of seizure.

"Yes," I say, looking away from the dog, "he is having convulsions. Just ignore him. Let's get back to: *Bucky? Gristle?*"

"Are you mocking my brother's name?"

I'm talking to Dr. Gristle. He's an old acquaintance of mine. We go way back. We share an intense interest in animals, and in making each other's life miserable. Right now, he is winning.

"You have a *brother*?" I ask, and shiver involuntarily. "Does that mean you have, like, parents and everything?"

"And everything, my lad. There is plenty more of me where I came from. And you are about to become acquainted with one of the finest members of my family line."

This is really bad. I am currently detained in a holding cell. There are two guards who work for Dr. Gristle, and the doctor himself, a sinister scientist with a specialization in two things — animal freakery, and me. The guards, who wear puffy white jumpsuits and white globular helmets, show zero signs of actual human life the whole time. They could be made of marble. The doctor works as a regular veterinarian in the full light of day, and on highly questionable biological/technological experiments when nobody's looking. Because some powerful people in the government or the army find his work very exciting, anyone who gets in Dr. Gristle's way finds himself in jeopardy.

Hi. My name is Zane. And I seem to get in his way a lot.

Dr. Gristle is blaming me for the fact that his carefully trained and programmed army of adorable killer macaque monkeys all de-enlisted at the same time and rode off on sea horses into the blue-green sunset of the WildArea. I happen to be the only human who could witness it. And while, strictly speaking, I was not responsible for the chain of events . . . it was a pretty darn cool chain all the same.

This is the type of thing that really sets the guy off.

"Where am I going?" I ask, reasonable enough. Last time I transgressed, I was sentenced to two months lockdown in my room. It wasn't a great laugh, but it wasn't Devil's Island, either. Clearly it didn't rehabilitate me, so I'm expecting the heat turned up. Maybe this time I'll have to spend two months in the bathroom.

"You're going . . . out," Dr. Gristle says with a wide, demented grin. Really, it's the only kind of grin he has.

"Out?" I ask. "Out where?"

I've got him irritated already, and I'm not even trying. Yet.

"What does it matter, out where? Isn't *out* bad enough?"

Right. I don't know what it's like elsewhere, but where I come from, the people look at the great outdoors like it is something to be scraped off your shoes no matter what part of it you've stepped in. We have playing fields just for show, while everyone plays on synthetic playing fields indoors. You can live in a community of a hundred thousand people but you would be lucky to run into two of them while walking your dog. And when you did, they'd give you a pity look, because only losers and outcasts are forced to spend any time with fresh air and green grass.

So being sent out is capital punishmentish.

Except not for me.

"Okay, sign me up, chief, I'm going out." I look around for my constant companion, but don't see him. "Where's Hugo? He loves it outside."

"Firstly, I am *Dr.* Chief. Secondly, don't be so confident until you get there and see. And thirdly, Hugo is not going anywhere. A person doesn't get sent to prison with all his creature comforts, after all."

Hugo is more than just a creature comfort. He can communicate with me, so he's man's best friend more than most dogs are.

The doctor is laughing. That's not a regular part of his evil loon toolbox.

"Why are you laughing?" I ask.

"I just realized what I said . . . about creature comforts. The dog, and all . . . creatures . . . that was very clever of me."

He's the life of a party nobody else ever attends.

His laughter is actually accelerating. I shiver again.

"Just send me to jail, will you?" I plead.

—◆—

"It's not jail, Zane," my mother says a few minutes later. "Honestly, you are so dramatic."

"That's right," my father adds. "It's much more like camp. Remember when you went to camp all those summers?"

My parents are not here with me. I am seeing them on a televisual screen, kind of like my one call from the police station. Not that it matters much — even if we were all at home, we would be talking to each other through screens and speakers and gadgets. Mom is famous for being a local

Newsmama, and Dad is famous for being That Voice over the radiowaves. But they are my units, and I have to love them. I think I clicked it in a user agreement at some point.

"Dad, I never went to a camp outdoors," I remind him. "They weren't camps, they were software. Even that alleged *sports camp* turned out to be a helmet with electrodes that you trapped me in for two weeks. I never even left the house. My head shrank and I got bald patches."

"Well, this will be a real camp," my mother chimes in. "And maybe it will install in you some of the discipline we have always tried, unsuccessfully, to install in you."

"Maybe if you tried *installing* it while being in the same room with me, it might take root."

My father is not amused. "Are you getting saucy with your mother?"

"Sorry for being saucy, Mother," I say. "But I really don't understand why I have to be subjected to Dr. Gristle's ideas about improving me."

"Don't you think the doctor knows best?" she asks.

"He's a *veterinarian*, for crying out loud. And a lunatic one at that."

"Name-calling won't help with your behavioral problem now, will it, Zane?" my father wants to know.

"Well, I don't know. Let's try some more and see. *Psycho! Mental Case! Doctor Bananas!* Hey, I don't know about you guys, but I feel like I'm definitely getting better."

They both glare at me through the screen.

"I apologize for being saucy," I say.

"Better," they say.

"Now, tell me where I'm going, please?"

"We're not allowed."

"You are about to turn over your only child to the care of a person called Bucky Gristle. And you can't even tell me where I'm going?"

"The doctor asked us not to," my mother says.

"Fine. Let me talk to Hugo. He's with you now, right?"

My parents giggle at me. Then my father stops short. "He wants to confer with the dog. He's not even incarcerated yet and he's showing signs of mental disarrangement."

"Right," I say. "So tell me."

"Okay, it's a kind of ranch, labor camp, not-quite-penal-colony kind of a thing for lads with an overabundance of friskiness and an underabundance of respect for authority."

That is, by a long way, the coolest thing anybody has ever said about me.

"You will work hard, work with animals, tire yourself out, and come back to us in no mood for any more of your hijinks. That's the theory anyway."

I am so going to shred that theory.

"Okay," I say, anxious to get on to our little adventure. "I guess it's good-bye, hijinks. I might not involve myself in any jinks of any height whatsoever, if this works out."

"That's a good start." My father, That Voice, actually does a goofy little fist pump of encouragement, which brings his wristwatch into view. "Holy cow," he says, "I've got a broadcast to prepare."

Which triggers my Newsmama to look at her watch. "Holy cow," she says.

Not wanting to disturb our religious cattle theme, I say my own "Holy cow!"

The two of them shuffle around there on the screen, gathering stuff up and straightening here and there. It is rare to see them both on the same screen together, and it's almost like the thing isn't big enough for them both. They jostle.

"Be good," my mother says, stopping and remembering me. "Honestly, son, just do your work, keep your head down, don't make a fuss. The time will pass, and then you can come home and start over fresh."

"I'll be so fresh my expiration date will be, like, a hundred and fifty years from now."

"It'll be a growing experience," my father says.

"I'll be massive," I say.

Their deadlines are getting to them now and they aren't really noticing what I'm saying.

"Be good," they say, touching hands flat to the screen in a mimey way that looks more like I am being shoved away. "Be good. Be smart."

"Be-elzebub," I say, putting my palm flat to the screen, pushing back, waiting for them to be gone.

Can you believe I already actually miss them? I deserve what I get, really.

I remove my hand slowly from the screen.

"Hi." It's Hugo's scruffy white head googling at me now.

"Hugo," I say, happy at seeing him, sad at realizing I won't be seeing him in person. "Man, I am so going to miss you."

"Can I have your bed?"

He's just being brave. He's really going to miss me.

"No, you can't have my bed."

"Stupid cat sleeps on it all the time. Now he thinks just because he sprayed your pillow it's all his. I think while you are away, I should assume ownership and control of your room and all your possessions, including meals. I'll be great at it; your parents will hardly even notice you're gone."

"They will notice. You're shorter than me."

"Who's shorter than you?" Dr. Gristle asks, sweeping into the room. "Who are you talking to, Zane?" He comes around to check out the screen.

Hugo has picked up on it and dashed out of sight.

"Were you listening in?" I ask, indignant.

"Certainly I was. This is an interrogation room, after all; they're always subject to surveillance."

"Do all veterinarian practices contain surveillance rooms?" I ask.

He grits his teeth at me. He would probably say it was a smile, but he'd be lying. "All the ones that are worth anything. Who were you talking to?"

"I was talking to my parents, saying good-bye like you arranged."

He grabs his chin, squeezes hard as if he's interrogating himself. He points at me sharply then. "You are not taller than your parents."

Dr. Gristle does not know that I can actually communicate with Hugo. I can also communicate with loads of other animals, ironically made possible by the doctor himself when he injects these special Gristle chips into them as part of his experiments. For some reason I can receive their thoughts over my Gizzard™ handheld communicator, with the earpiece making Hugo's voice clear as day in my head.

The Doc knows I have something special going for me. He just doesn't know what. He sure would like to.

"When my mother isn't wearing heels, I'm taller than her now."

He is still pointing at me. "Oh," he says. He wants to say more, challenge me more, but short of bringing my mother in for a measurement, he's stuck.

"Shouldn't we get moving?" I say to him.

"Pretty anxious, aren't you, for someone who is about to experience a very tough regime and a lot of outdoorsiness?"

He says the word *outdoorsiness* as if it's supposed to make me cry.

"I am ready to pay my debt to society, sir."

He leans down close. I truly hate it when he does this.

His teeth and forehead and hair are all really big and blindingly bright, and he always smells like parts of animals, but never like the neck of a kitten or anything.

"You could start by sharing your gift with me, your secret. If you did that, maybe some of your punishment wouldn't even be necessary."

I pause. He has turned his back to the screen to face me full on. Over his shoulder I catch Hugo sneaking back into cam range. He is shaking his big round face at me, no, and it is just so dumb that he feels he has to tell me not to tell the doctor the secret, I cannot control myself.

"Well, duh," I say in disgust.

Dr. Gristle pulls back sharply from me. "Fine," he hisses. "Obstinate *and* rude. I'd say you are going to the ranch at just the right time. You have much to learn, my friend. And Bucky Gristle is not as open-minded and tolerant as his brother."

I would very much like to say something snappy right now. Unfortunately, my throat has gone so dry I cannot speak, with the thought of what awaits me.

BRUTES, BRATS & BUCKY

The first thing you notice when you approach the ranch is the bone-dry heat of the place. And the vast hugeness. It doesn't seem to begin or end; it's just all here.

"Is this it?" I ask Dr. Gristle as I rub and rub at my eyes. The brightness is zapping me after spending ages in the darkened back of his vehicle. It's as if the whole world at this moment is made from a graft of his blazing forehead.

"This is it, yes," he says. He gestures vaguely. "That way."

I look that way. "There seems to be a great deal of space between us and *that* way, Doctor."

"Yes, so you'd better get started."

"Or you could just take me the rest of the way."

"What, and spoil the experience for you? That is what you are here for, right? Experience?"

"I thought I was here because I am a constant pain in your backside."

He is already backing away from me, toward his vehicle. "Oh," he says, holding up two open hands like a big surprise, "that's it. That's why I won't be taking you farther, the backside thing, I almost forgot." Then he gets deadly serious. "Good luck, Zane. And try to get the point this time, before you get yourself into serious trouble."

Serious trouble. Yes, he is just that funny all the time.

I wave in exaggerated friendliness as he speeds off, then wheel in the direction of my destination. To find . . . nothing. Nothing but heat and dry and lots more nothing.

I am pretty alone, I must say. I start walking.

The sun is stronger than I have ever experienced it before. There is nowhere for shade, not so much as a scrub of bush to crawl under. Good thing I like the outdoors. After a little while, walking, walking, watching the horizon do absolutely nothing, I stop. It is like a still picture, and no matter how much I walk, I don't appear to be one bit closer to anything, and nothing appears to be one bit different from ten or twenty minutes ago. I come up with a very clever idea and start running. I took up running a while back and found that I was pretty not-bad at it. Every time I ran, I appeared to get places. Running makes sense here.

Soon after the run starts, I find myself sitting on the ground. No, not sitting. If you use your elbows, does that count as sitting? How 'bout if you use your back, and the back of your head? My goodness, I have never felt anything like this heat. The skin on my face is starting to crisp, so I flop over onto my nose.

I have been left out here with no provisions, no tools, or anything other than the clothes on me and the Gizzard™ strapped to my arm. Last time I was punished, all communication was denied me for two months. But since that incarceration was within the cold, comforting walls of my own home, that was permissible. This time, though, because I am going to be far away from loved ones and left out to die in the desert and all, my parents put their feet down and insisted I be allowed to keep my Gizzard™ so they could be in touch.

As I think this thought, I attempt a small tear droppage out of one eye. Mission incomplete, however, as I have evaporated.

So I buzz my father.

I don't get my father. Instead, on the small screen of my Gizzard™ I get the somehow-still-big gumball of a head of my neighbor Fuze, who is one year younger than me and a thousand years nuttier. Her full name is Lori Fuze, but I always call her Fuze. It helps with distance because she doesn't get the territory thing at all.

"Zane!" She always speaks with more enthusiasm than any situation calls for.

"Fuze," I say flatly. It's the only way. "Are you in my father's studio?"

"Yes!" she says. "Where are you?"

"I'm lying on my face a million miles from civilization or a drink of water."

"Oh, you are *not* lying on your face. I can see your face."

"Yes, and why can you see my face? What are you doing in my father's studio? What are you doing in my house?"

Before she can say anything, Hugo flies past the screen like a speeding, rabid white cloud. "Help!" he says.

"What's wrong with Hugo?" I ask.

"Nothing. He's great. We're becoming best pals!"

"Help!" Hugo says, flying past in the other direction. He's got a lot of spring in his leap, I have to say.

"Why are you becoming best pals? Why are you there?"

"Your father hired me. With you away, he needed some-body to come over and pick up the slack, do all the stuff that you would be doing."

"I didn't leave any slack, Fuze. I don't do anything, so there's no need —"

"These poor neglected animals certainly can't take care of themselves, now can they?"

I am tempted to tell her that they can. In fact —

"Your room is the coolest place on earth," she says.

She has never been in my room before, and that is no accident. Lori Fuze is a very nice person, just a little scary and in possession of ideas I don't have and will never be likely to have.

Here comes one now.

"Your dad is the nicest man," she says. "He's a big, sweet friendly thing like Santa Claus. And he has a voice like a president. He could be *president*."

"Don't go in my room, Fuze."

"I'm sorry, sir, but you didn't hire me, so I don't take my orders from you."

Now I really *am* facedown in the desert. This is so frustrating.

"Where is my father?" I ask.

"I don't know."

"Does he know you're there?"

"I'm sorry, sir, but I only answer to the boss."

"Where is my mother?"

"How would I know that?"

"Is this fun for you?"

"Well, I didn't mean for it to be, but, yes, I suppose it is now."

"Could you kindly have my father get in touch with me when he gets back? Passing on messages is within your job description, isn't it?"

"I don't know. I'll have to run that by the boss when he gets in."

I click her off. It is the only thing remotely like a feeling of power I can manage because right now I feel like I have less power in more directions than I have ever had in my essentially powerless life. I feel the sun beating on the back of my head, smell the dry dirt of earth as I breathe it in. But I don't move.

Then I feel tugging. At my arms, my legs, my sides.

I raise my head carefully and look all around me.

I am surrounded by a gang of eight chubby little prairie dogs.

I have no idea if they are chipped or not, but I say what you say in a situation like this: "What are you doing?"

"We are tying you up." Only one is speaking. He's at my feet.

"No, you're not," I say, and roll over onto my hip. They only work harder, scurrying around, trying to attach my shoelaces to a couple of small rocks, trying to attach my belt to a scrubby viney bush that looks like a garnish. I feel like Gulliver in Lilliput. Only you wouldn't feel like scooping up the Lilliputians and giving them a squeeze, but these guys you probably would.

"Sorry," I say, "but you don't appear to me to even have the basic equipment for tying."

Indignant, the whole group stands upright at once. They show me their impressive little hands in front of their impressive little bellies, dangling their fingers like they are waiting for manicures.

"Sorry again," I say, "I didn't mean to insult your skills. Lovely mitts you've got there." I sit up now, leaning forward and hanging on to my knees. They scramble and huddle together to face me, arranged according to height. They all look the same.

"Why would you want to tie me up anyway?"

"The big animals told us to."

"What big animals? How do they know me, anyway? And why would they want you to tie me up? You probably don't even have the right guy."

They all start barking at one another. It's quite a thing, the squeaky, yippy thing that makes a prairie dog a squirty version of doglike. But they don't seem to mean it to be as cute as it is.

"He thinks we're stupid, he thinks we're stupid," is the gist of what I can get of the exchange.

"I do *not* think you're stupid. You may be stupid, but I don't know you yet, so I will reserve judgment. Which brings me back to the question of how you know me . . ."

"Everybody knows you, Zane," the prairie dogs answer. "We've known about you for a while now. We even saw you coming from quite a distance. Nobody knows for sure what you are, but we know you sure are something."

I sit up a little taller. Closer to the dangerous sun, but hey, how often do you get this kind of reception from strangers?

"Cool," I say. "I am known, far and wide."

"Yes, you are," says the pudgy little leader. "And the big animals want to stomp your brains out."

"What?" I ask, temperature now spiking dangerously. "What? Why? Me?"

"Well, the big animals, they're always angry about something."

"That doesn't explain stomping me. Why should they want to stomp me? Animals usually like me. You don't want to stomp me, right?"

"That's because I'm not them. That's how these guys react to stuff. Because they are big animals. They stomp. That's what they do. They get angry, and they stomp."

"Me?"

"Uh-huh. First there is the regular ordinary crazy anger. Then there's the fact that they especially don't trust any human that has a chip in him. They figure you are some kind of Gristle fink."

"I am no kind of Gristle! I am the anti-Gristle!"

He is shaking his fuzzy little head. "All I can tell you is, the words *butt* and *kick* are being tossed around the trough at a much greater rate than usual. And the usual rate is already quite high."

"Ah, puke."

"Yeah," he says sympathetically. "Puke, indeed. That's what I'd do, for starters, if I were you."

"Thanks. But as you are clearly not going to succeed at tying me up, could you — what is your name, by the way?"

"James."

"Okay, James. Do you think you could lead me to a drink of water?"

"Sure I can," he says.

James is the most accommodating prairie dog I have ever met. And considering he came out here on a mission to abduct me and leave me for dead, it's even more impressive. The whole posse of them sets out ahead of me like a gang — or a funeral procession — and I follow.

By the time my little entourage arrives at the promised watering place, I am ready to drop to my knees and drink dirt.

Which is nearly what I have to do.

"Here we are," says James.

"Where we are?" says me. They have marched me over a great distance, under a great sun that looks like it wants to set, only we keep following it. The landscape has barely changed except for the fact that the parched ground is now dotted with holes that are suspiciously James-size.

Every one of those prairie dogs disappears down a hole, and in a few minutes each adorable, punchable little face comes up dripping glorious water droplets.

Is it wrong to want to lick the face of a prairie dog?

"James," I say, wobbly now, "are you telling me the only water is . . ."

"Yeah," he says brightly, "wait till you see it. We have a whole town down there, all these connecting tunnels and food storage and water . . . oh. Oh, right, the size thing. Hold on." He disappears again.

Once again, I do as he says. I try to hold on. I actually reach out, grasp at — what, a tree? A ladder? A nurse? I flail, and I fall.

James pops back up, and I am watching him sideways, from my sideways position. Bless him, he has his tiny little mitts cupped together, trying to bring me a drink. There are probably six molecules of water in there.

"You can't drink lying on your side," he says. "It doesn't work. You gotta sit up."

I cannot sit up. I can just about manage to stare at him blankly.

He shrugs and laps up the water out of his own hands.

⊶⬤⊷

It is a pleasant sensation. I am not upright, but I am not exactly lying on anything, either. I am not moving, but I am not staying still, either.

I see the big rough-hewn wooden archway of the facility passing overhead against a dusky purple sky.

PRIMEVAL KENIEVAL RANCH, it reads, burnt into the woodwork.

I finally look down. I am being carried along by a sort of parade float of eight strong prairie dudes.

Until I am not. All as one they do a heave-ho and

dump me on my side. It's not a long fall, I have to say, but I feel it.

"Thanks," I tell James, who is nose-to-nose with me now.

"I'm not so sure thanks is the right response to this, but okay," he says. He extends his hand.

With some effort I reach out and shake it. James has a surprisingly firm grip.

As if they are controlled by the same single puppetmaster, all the prairie dogs straighten up at once. Same posture, same inquiring look. Then, as one, they blast off back in the direction from which they came.

"Good luck!" calls James.

"Thanks!" I call back.

"Stop thanking me!" he cries. "It's making me feel guilty."

It isn't exactly thunderous, a stampede of PDs, but it's impressive in its own way.

"Zane, Zane, Zany!" comes the call that makes me nearly shed my own skin. I roll on the ground and look to see a man scurrying toward me. Even from a distance, in the semidark, in my state of dehydrated dementia, I can sense this is not a stable man headed my way.

"Zane, Zany," he says, arriving to help me to my feet, even though my feet don't want me. "Bucky, Bucky Gristle here. How are you?"

"Well, to tell you the truth, Bucky-Bucky —"

"One Bucky, Zane. One. There is only one Bucky."

I already recognize this as fantastic news.

"Sorry. But to tell you the truth, Bucky, if I don't get some water, I am dead."

"Of course," he says. "Of course, of course, of course." And he yanks me hard, as if I were a person with a normal amount of fluid in his body.

He leads me almost all the way into the log-cabiny structure nearest to us, but not quite. We stop outside.

"What is this?" I ask, waving toward the long and low wooden container of water in front of me.

"Well, a little later it's your bath. But right now it's your drink. Unless you would like to flip them around and do it the other way, which is perfectly fine by me."

Without even intending to, I drop to my knees. Without even intending to, I lurch forward, my face in the water, and start slurping. All completely involuntary on my part; my body has decided to shove my useless brain out of the way and make the decisions for us. For the best, I believe, and something that should probably happen more often.

Shortly thereafter, I am slumped in a big leather wing chair. I inhale deeply and start coughing like a wolf. My chest hurts and my lungs feel like they are filled with ice cream.

"That is why it's not advisable to pass out while submerged in water," Bucky Gristle says, forcing me forward and giving my back several robust poundings. "You ain't much of a physical specimen, boy."

By the time I straighten back up, I feel a bit better, though my back now hurts, to go along with my sun-crispy face and hands.

"There," Bucky says. "That's better." He walks around from behind me, circles his giant shiny wood desk, and stands on the other side for me to see. He clinks.

"Are you wearing spurs?" I ask.

"Yes, sir, I am."

It's hard to believe this is Dr. Gristle's brother. I don't see the resemblance. He's about a foot shorter, just about my height, with a round face, black hair, and major sideburns. His face is lined and browned and smacks of "outdoors," just as much as his brother's does of "outer space." He looks as if he is making an effort to be bowlegged, and holds his arms out away from his body like he's ready to quick-draw at all times. I don't really know yet what to make of him, but am relieved so far with the lack of connection to the good doctor's bad aura.

Then he lays the ol' electro-grin on me.

"Yeek!" I actually scream, recoiling in my chair.

"What's wrong, Zane?" he asks, his concern apparently genuine.

"Sorry," I say. "Flashback."

"Well," says Bucky Gristle, allowing himself to fall

expertly backward into his own big leather chair, "that is why you are here, ain't it?"

"It is?" I ask.

"It is," he answers. "You got demons, boy. And this is the place where a boy comes to be rid of his demons and learn to become a contributing member of the right kind of society. As I understand, you yourself have quite a bit to contribute to society. Am I right, Zany?"

I am so distracted right now I don't even get around to asking him to stop calling me that. I have to stare, and it's taking up all my attention. Because hanging above Bucky's head is a bison head so large and menacing and fantastic-looking it has to have come from a workshop and not from a real animal.

"Oh," Bucky says, casting a glance up over his own shoulder. He acts slightly surprised, as if, shucks, this ol' thing is not the first thing every visitor wants to know about. If that beast were a truck, Bucky could be his hood ornament.

"That big beautiful fella is Primeval Kenieval, the buffalo this very place is named for. He was our first reha-bilitation project. Mean and murderous as anything on four legs when we got him. My goodness, I loved that critter. That chair you're sitting on is made of ol' PK. Mine, too. I do miss him."

"So you're going to make furniture out of me when you're finished, huh?"

Bucky scowls, which is a lot less scary than his smile.

"I heard about this *smart sense of humor* of yours," he says. When he says the important words there, he tries to make the quotation marks in the air. But he does it in what must be the cowboy way, using all five fingers on each hand as if he is checking invisible air grapefruits for ripeness.

"Sorry," I say. "I will try to keep the *smartness* to a minimum while I'm here."

"Good," he says, lightening up. I think he's swayed by my grapefruiting. "Because, young Zane, this is what we are dedicated to here. We bring together damaged emotional brutes like the aforementioned Primeval Keneival here, and work them alongside damaged emotional brats like yourself, and ultimately break — that is, rehabilitate — all those great and small creatures into one fantastic, broken, fantastic, functional, rehabilitated, powerful force of workitudability . . . and fantasticate everybody in the process."

There is some time now, as the smoke clears and we find ourselves staring at each other. I can only assume that my face looks as puzzled as his does.

"You're going to work the wise guy right out of me, aren't you?" I ask.

"You betcha," he says, the grin leaping out at me like a taser. "Now let's get you bunked in."

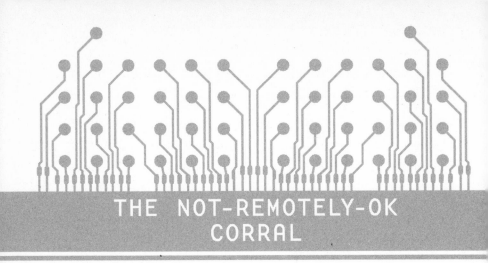

THE NOT-REMOTELY-OK CORRAL

At first, it seems like "bunking in" is going to mean being stabled right in with the animals. I had a sort of fun vision of a *bunkhouse* from the days when there was something like a cowboy life that people actually wanted to live, in the days before it became strictly a correctional idea.

But then Bucky Gristle leads me, with my scratchy blanket and a pillow sporting very visible yellow drool stains, right to the unmistakable lodgings where all the slippers are shaped like hooves.

As soon as we swing into the Hotel Hee-Haw, I panic with the notion of having one of Primeval Keneival's offspring for a roommate.

"Oh, goodness, no." Bucky laughs when I guess at it. "That would be chaotic and vicious. I would never get away with that."

I feel better.

Though we have not entirely managed to sidestep chaotic and vicious.

The place goes mental. Every beast in the building reacts at once. I hear grunts and snorts, animals bashing themselves against walls and gates. It is like there is a great shake-up, somebody picking the place right off the ground and jerking it around to throw us all into a storm of thrashing and spitting and noise. I try to decipher what they're saying, but I get nothing. Not because they are animals, but because they are *athlete* animals. I don't do any better with football players.

"Is this some kind of greeting?" I shout to Bucky.

"Yes, yes, they are very happy to smell you."

"Well, happy to smell you, too," I say to the crowd. We pass a stall, and a chestnut horse with the Gristle family smile shoves his face into the bars in a wild bite attempt. Bucky laughs.

"Scamps," he says. "A bunch of scamps, we have here."

"Now that I've seen the scampery," I say nervously, "can we leave here and put me to bed? I have had a very long and exhausting —"

"Here we are," Bucky hoots.

We are standing in front of a stable, door flung wide. There is straw all over the floor. There is a dim yellow light hanging from the ceiling, and another one propped on a small table next to what looks like a bench covered in more straw, growing out from one wall.

"Can't we see all this stuff tomorrow, Bucky? I really am tired."

"Tired? How fortunate." He gives me a nudge, which in my weakened state sends me deep into the stall. "Goodness, that was easy," he says when I pivot to look at him. He slings the barn door shut. Then he comes up and looks at me through the bars of the top half. "These are your living quarters while you are here." I hear the bolt slam shut.

"The lock appears to be on the wrong side of my bedroom door," I say.

"Call the front desk. They will . . . oh, wait, I *am* the front desk. Get a very important good night's sleep, Zany," he says, walking off.

I go to the bars. "I am not Zany!" I shout.

"Maybe not yet. . . ." he calls. Then he yodels.

"He yodels," I say.

I make my way back to my *bed*, and even alone I cannot help making the ten-finger quotation sign at my *bed*. But right now I could sleep on the backs of a team of porcupines — which I should probably not say out loud around here because I imagine it could be arranged.

I take my drool pillow and my sandpaper blanket and lay myself down on the straw *bedding*. . . .

"Stop that, Zane!" I say to my quotation hands.

And, you know, I am that tired. I am, very shortly, comfortable. I believe I can even enjoy this, in a back-to-nature way, the night air on my skin, the fullness of animal air in my nose.

Boom!

My wall has just attacked me, and I crash to the floor. I sit there, stunned, looking back at the bed as if it's haunted and against me.

"I am so going to kick your butt from here to the moon and back again," says my wall.

My wall has a very deep voice and snorts a lot. Exactly the same as I'm guessing my neighbor does on the other side of the wall.

Boom! comes the response from the opposite wall behind me.

"Not if I kick it first," says Snorty Wall Two.

"We could share," says Wall One.

"Yes, we could. That would be fun."

Harmony. Peace and cooperation. That's the stuff.

I don't dare get back up on the bunk. The straw on the floor is just as fresh and golden and fluffy as the stuff up there anyway. And my friend has been kind enough to also kick down the reading materials that have been left for me on the little night table that I now realize is probably a milking stool.

I have not been left with the Bible. At least not *that* Bible. There are several books here, all with the author name *Gristle* on the spine. In fact, one of them is called simply *SPINE*, by a certain Bucky Gristle. The full title is *SPINE: How to Have One, How to Snap One, and How to Stop Crying About It*. And one by Dr. Gary Gristle called *IF YOUR*

PETS COULD TALK, with the subtitle *They'd Beg for More Gristle.*

The Gristle boys' mother must be awfully proud.

Now I've done it. I've thought about them having a mother and won't get to sleep for hours.

—•—

I wake up, on the floor in the straw, after a miserable night sleeping, not sleeping, picturing the ghostly grin of Ma Gristle, and absorbing threatening grunts and neighs around me. The buzzing of my Gizzard™ ends the night for good.

"What?" I say into it.

It's Hugo. He's managed to work himself onto my desk chair and get my computer camera to send his charming wiry mug to me here.

"It's me," he says, a little anxiously.

"I can see it's you. This is amazing. I am away from home for the first time, in pretty rough circumstances, and my dog stays in touch while my parents don't."

"Well, I need you, and they don't."

"Thanks, I'm touched. What's wrong?"

"It's that Fuze person. She's what's wrong."

"She sure is, isn't she?"

"Yes. She's practically running the place. She's decided that my teeth aren't white enough so now I only get dry dog food because it's supposed to be good for the choppers."

"So you'll have a dazzling smile."

"I have a set menu, Zane — you know that. You can't just change a set menu. How's somebody supposed to live on nothing but dry? Huh? Then she decides I'm not relieving myself with the frequency or volume she would like — well, duh, hello, dry food! — so you know what she's started giving me, for a *treat*? Little bowls of prune juice mixed with beef gravy. Hey, I see you. Stop laughing."

"Well, come on, Hugo — you don't have to drink it."

"Yes I do. It's got beef gravy in it!"

"I can see where that would be hard to resist."

"I need you to come home, right now."

"Ah, Hugo, I am essentially, you know, in jail here. I don't think they let you go home just because your dog is having a toilet issue."

"I am *not* having a toilet issue!"

I'm laughing harder now because he's just so cute when he's flustered. Then, there's a commotion. I see scuffling on the screen and Hugo sort of squeals.

"What are you doing up here, you crazy little dog," Fuze shrills, wrestling Hugo away from the computer. "Hey, Zane — what are you doing here?"

"It's my room, Fuze, I belong here. Not you, though. I told you to stay out of my room."

"Oh, but you didn't mean that. How am I ever supposed to be you, if I can't be in your room?"

"Don't be me. I'll be me. And what's wrong with my dog? He seems very upset."

"Oh, that's just a little problem we call Hugo No-Go."

"Grrrr. Rowr. Rowr. Grrr."

"Hugo," she says, looking down and swatting at the area of her legs. "Stop, that's Mommy's Achilles tendon. That hurts Mommy."

Mommy?

"Mommy?"

"Yes, I'm his mommy, and he's my little Hugo No-Go, but we're working on that."

Hugo leaps up now, his rear paws on her lap, his front paws on the desktop. His face is pressed so close to the camera I can see all the way up his nose into his brain. Which is badly inflamed.

"Zane? Zane?"

"Listen, little No-Go, it sounds like Mommy has everything under control. I have enough to deal with here, with giant beasts lining up to take turns kicking my body parts into whole new arrangements."

"I'll trade ya. I'll trade ya."

The door to my cage swings open.

"I have to go," I say. "Wish me luck. I'm actually a little worried about dying here."

"It's always me, me, me, huh, Zane?"

Fuze is about to say something when I switch her off.

"You are very unlikely to die here, Zane," Bucky Gristle says. "It hardly ever happens." He walks over and hands me my breakfast. It is a big tin plate with corned beef hash and baked beans all over it. It's all swimming around.

"Well, that's good to know," I say. I start shoveling some of the mush into my mouth and it tastes better than it looks. That is not a huge compliment, since it looks worse than whatever Hugo eats, wet or dry. But I'm starving, and probably needing whatever strength I can get.

"Twenty seconds," he says.

"Hmmm?" I ask with my mouth full.

"Fifteen seconds," he says. "Time's a-wastin'."

I really shovel at the food now. It's helpful that the consistency of the slop means chewing is not really necessary. It's less helpful that the stuff gets mushier with each contact and all I have is a fork and it's escaping me faster and faster.

"There ya go," Bucky says and snatches the plate out of my hand. My fork clatters to the floor, and as I go to pick it up, he walks out of the stall.

I look up to find Bucky crouched over, feeding the other three quarters of my breakfast to a grunting slobbering pig with no manners and a neck that could dam a decent-size river. He's got a sort of collar around that neck that looks like a bunch of red bricks all strung together.

"That's the stuff, piggy," Bucky says, slapping the pig on the neck. He stands up straight and flashes me the plate. "Look at that. Doesn't even need to be washed now."

I gag, wondering if in fact that was how the plate got cleaned before I ate off it.

The pig uncurls a massive squeal that sounds quite like he is having a good laugh at my expense.

"This ol' boy is going to be your playmate this morning," Bucky says of the pig. "His name is Pinkish Hugh, and he is needing a little bit of loving attention. I hear tell that you are very good with animals and loving attention, is that right?"

"I would say that is pretty accurate, yes."

Great. Time to bond.

Bucky leads the way, and we head out of the building into the yard. Pinkish Hugh and I walk side by side, as equals, a few steps behind Bucky.

"In case you were wondering, I was laughing at you back there," the pig says.

"Got it," I say.

"Just so you know."

"I do. With a name like Pinkish Hugh, I guess you know a lot about being laughed at, huh?"

He actually stops right there in his tracks. I turn to look at him.

"I am so kicking your butt," he snorts. "I'm very glad I get first crack at you."

"Sorry," I say. "I didn't mean anything."

We resume walking.

"Doesn't matter what you meant. Doesn't even matter if you said nothing at all. I'm stomping you."

"Why?"

"Feel like it."

"Oh. What's that thing strapped around your neck?"

"What do I look like, the Answer Pig?"

"Sorry."

"Don't worry about it. You're dead meat anyway. Thanks for the breakfast though."

Finally.

"Oh, you're welcome."

"Shut up. Anyway, my friends call me P-Hugh, so that's cooler."

"P-Hugh it is."

"I thought I told you to shut up. You're not my friend."

"I'd like to be."

"Oh, now you're just making it worse."

Shutting up is sounding like very good advice as we reach the far side of the yard and enter into another, smaller building.

"Right," says Bucky, clapping his hands together. "This is where you get started." He hands me a clipboard. On the first page is a sheet with P-Hugh's name on the top and a lot of boxes for writing figures. "I am going to leave you to it, but here is the sequence. That over there is the pig weigh crate."

It's a big blue-painted metal cage with two wheels at one end so you can lift the other and wheel it around. It's got a large circular gauge on top like if you were weighing fruit at the store.

"Then there's that." He walks me over to what appears to be a rubber mat surrounded by a fence. He flips a switch on a fence post, and the rubber mat starts moving. He pushes a lever forward and it goes faster, then he brings it back down again. There is an odometer to measure the distance.

"Lastly, there is this," he says, and walks me over to an oversize salad bowl with a lid. He removes the lid to reveal a heaping mound of what appears to be all the waste left from a restaurant over a weekend. He puts the lid back on.

"Now, Zane, you are to take ol' Pinkish here through his paces. He's got to be weighed, then he has to do his ten miles on the treadmill before he gets his delicious slop. Can't let him get lazy now, because he will. So you use this stick" — he hands me what looks like a cane with a nail on the end of it — "to remind him what's what."

I look over from Bucky to Hugh. I have never seen an angry pig before, so I don't have a lot to go on, but this looks like a furious, murderous pig. And he's saving it up for me.

"Don't you want to stay for a bit and show me the ropes?" I say as Bucky heads out.

"What ropes? It's all simple. You're supposed to be a very bright boy. So brighten the place up. There's lots else to do around here. I'll check on ya in a while."

He's gone, slamming the door in my face. I lean on the door for a few extra seconds.

I feel hot pig breath on the back of my thighs.

"Yes?" I ask.

"I'm sensitive about my weight," he says.

"Well, sure," I say, turning slowly and nodding sympathetically. "That's totally understand —"

"Are you calling me fat?"

"No! Of course I'm not. I just meant that anybody would feel the same —"

"You?"

"Me, what?"

"Sensitive about your weight?"

"Me, well, um. Sure."

"You are not weighing me, kid. That's for sure."

"But Bucky told me I have to. I have no choice."

"I'm not getting in there."

Rats. It seems highly unlikely that anything I will be asked to do on this penal farm will be easier than weighing the pig. I cannot fail at this, and I cannot start out by being intimidated by Pinkish Hugh.

"I'm afraid I'm going to have to make you get in that weigh crate, Hugh."

The laughing squeal sound is so large now, if you were on the outside of this building, you would think my task was not to weigh him, but to slaughter him.

"All right," I say, irritated now. "That's enough."

"I bite, you know," he informs me.

"Well, of course you do," I say. "This situation just wouldn't make any sense if you couldn't bite me."

"Are you saying you don't think I have a variety of other skills with which to give you a whipping? You think I need to bite you?"

"No, not at all. I'm certain that you are a very skilled pig, with many tools for whipping me, and . . . you know, you are a seriously disagreeable pig. What is your problem? Were you an unloved little suckling when you were a baby?"

I don't mean anything by it, really. Just trying to hold my ground.

He sniffs. "As a matter of fact, I was not the prize pig. My precious brothers were soooo . . . hey, shut up."

"Okay, fine, I'll shut up. Just get on the scale."

"Make me."

"You got it, porky."

I am so angry and frustrated, I just swing around behind him, get a running start, and slam into his backside with everything in me.

"You okay?" he asks, his snout near my snout now as I stay on all fours, attempting to fill my lungs with smelly, life-sustaining air.

"Just knocked the wind out of myself, that's all."

"Now I feel bad," the pig says, although I doubt he truly means it. "Tell you what — you weigh yourself first, then we can weigh me."

"Fine," I say, recognizing a good deal when I see one. I remain on all fours and crawl my way onto the floor of the weigh crate.

"Okay, what do I weigh?" I ask.

I hear the gate of the crate slam behind me, and the latch fall into place.

"Let me see now," P-Hugh says casually, circling around to get closer to the reading. "It says here you weigh exactly . . . ten stupids. No, sorry, that's ten point three stupids."

"What's going on here?" Bucky yells from the doorway.

I cannot say this is the proudest moment of my life.

"Um, I fell," I say.

"You fell? Into the weigh crate? And locked the gate behind you? My goodness, boy, can it be true that you have been outwitted and humiliated by a pig?"

Wow. I feel a lot worse now. I imagine this is about as low as a guy can go, and I have achieved it within minutes of my first morning.

Pig squeals. Which is only right. I'd be squealing my head off if I were him.

"Since you put it that way, Bucky . . . I'm going to stick with 'I fell.'"

"Right," says Bucky, clearly disgusted. "You are going to be a lot more work than I bargained for, kid."

"Sorry," I say.

Apparently, sorry is not enough. And apparently, I have not already reached as low as a guy could go.

I feel a bump. Then a shift as I find myself leaning forward and bumping my face on the cage. Then we are moving.

"What are you doing?" I ask.

"I'm showing you off," Bucky says.

Before I can say rats or puke, we are ratsy pukey out the door and into the sunlight of the courtyard. Bucky reverses out, turns around, and drives me toward the pens and paddocks and fields of the ranch.

"Suddenly you seem like a lot more fun," says P-Hugh, trotting alongside me like a police escort.

I am covering my head with my hands and probably making myself look even more embarrassing, but I don't care. This moment just has to pass, and while I have to be here for it, I don't have to witness it. If I don't look, it will all be over before I know it.

"Zane," Bucky says, "I'd like you to meet the team."

"I don't think this is the best time for me to meet the team," I say. "Maybe later when I have had more time to —"

I have no effect. I am meeting the team whether I like it or not. For their part, it seems the team likes it very much.

I hear lots of the same animal noises I heard on my entry into the stables last night. And a lot more. Clearly what I am listening to is a combination of mocking laughter and violent rage. I have to peek over my hands now as Bucky wheels me down a dirt lane, between pens of different animals. Horses and sheep. Cows and goats. Bulls. Alpaca. I see, in the hills just beyond the pens, dozens of large, crazy hares darting around, and it may be paranoia at this point, but I'm sure I can hear them making fun of me.

"Now, boys and girls," Bucky says, "this is our new guest, Zane. You will be working closely with him, and I want you to show him all the respect he deserves."

As we pass a fence, one bull shows me all the respect I deserve by charging right into the post in an effort to get at me, snorting a great batch of bull spittle all the way into my cage.

"Can we go home now?" I ask Bucky, my hands back over my face, which is exactly where they belong. "I think I've met the team pretty well for now, and gotten the ball rolling, respect-wise."

"Sure thing," Bucky says, angling back the way we came. "You and Pinkish still have a long day of work together. Followed by his bath, of course."

"Of course," I say.

"Of course," squeals Pinkish.

SLAPSTICK

Pigs have a great sense of humor. They love a laugh. They also love food and baths. They seem to love most things.

Except me. Pinkish Hugh took every opportunity to butt me, to squash me against walls. To stick his foul squib of a tail in my eye during bath time. And to bite me. And bite me. And step on my feet with his surprisingly sharp and unsurprisingly weight-bearing hooves. And bite me. It was as if he had the exact figure on how many bites of spare rib I'd had in my life and he was going to pay me back for each and every one of them.

It's like I lost my gift with the animals overnight. I have to get it back, to get these animals back on my side, or life here in jail will not be the holiday I'd hoped it would be.

"Good morning," Bucky says, louder than the rooster who's been crowing right straight into my cell for the last half hour.

"Good morning," I say. I am lying on my bedlike slab;

the wall banging of my neighbors is already less overpowering than the exhaustion I feel.

Bucky opens the door and walks over to me with my breakfast. The rooster walks right in with him, like he's trained.

"Roo-oooh-oooh-oohh!" the bird crows, staring straight up at me.

"I heard you," I snap. "All twenty-five times. I am neither deaf nor stupid."

"He saw the pig trap you in the cage," Bucky reminds me.

"I trapped myself in the cage," I insist, rather pointlessly.

I sit with my tin plate in my lap and stare down into yesterday's breakfast. Really, even if I ate the food and then lost it again, it would look pretty much exactly like this.

"Hash and beans again," I say.

"Hash and beans," he says, clapping.

"Don't I get to drink with breakfast?" I ask.

"Now, Zane, you know your drink is outside, when you are finished."

"Right. In my bath."

"Correct."

"My cold, out-in-the-open bath."

"That's the one. Rainwater. Best thing for ya, inside and out. So, how do you feel after your first day on the ranch?"

"Like it's my forty-first day on the ranch." I shift a little where I sit, and feel every muscle pull in a different direction from what it usually does.

"Roo-oo-roo-oo!"

"I'm awake, you stupid bird. I don't sleep sitting up like you."

"He's just doing his job, Zane," Bucky says, wounded, as if I have insulted him personally.

"Sorry. I guess I'm a little tired and achy this morning."

"Ya, well, ol' Hughy is a lot of pig, I have to say."

"Yes. He is a whole lot of pig."

"Wait till the hard work starts," he says.

"Yeah," I say, "wait till —"

"Twenty seconds!"

"What?"

"Ten seconds!"

I start shoveling the food again, and again it gets thinner and more elusive as I work at it.

"Done," Bucky says, confiscating the plate when I am so obviously not done.

"Okay," I say as he takes my breakfast to a pail just outside the door and starts scraping. "What's my assignment this morning?"

"This fine beautiful morning," he says, putting an arm around my shoulders, "you have one of the finest tasks in the world."

I wait for him to elaborate, but he opts for show-and-tell

instead. We get to the big door that swings out to the yard, and find . . . "A horse," I say.

"Pony," Bucky corrects me. "This guy is technically a pony. And he's a fat little pony, too, as you may have noticed."

I did sort of notice that, but figured it might just be a pony thing, a bit of a potbelly. I go up and pat the belly gently.

"How would you like a horseshoe tattoo for luck?" the pony asks me. "Pat my belly again, and I'll give you one right in the middle of your forehead."

"He's in bad need of some regular exercise," Bucky says, walking up and patting the belly just like I did, only with more slap.

"Everything he does, you get blamed for," pony says.

"What's his name?" I ask Bucky.

"Mercury."

"Is he really fast?"

"No, just his temper."

Mercury's little neigh-laugh sounds flattered. I start yearning for the good old days with the hateful pink pig.

"What is this thing?" I ask Bucky, going up to the necklace of bricks that Mercury wears, just like P-Hugh and all the larger beasts of the ranch seem to.

"Oh, them things, don't worry about them. That's just a part of the very sophisticated apparatus we employ around here, to make the animals as happy and healthy and vigorous and productive as they can be."

I look at the necklace. It looks heavy. And tight, like it's embedded into the pony's neck. I think I can even hear a faint humming coming off of it.

"Yes," I say, "but what is it?"

Bucky doesn't appear to care for follow-up questions.

"I am a ranch man, for pete's sake. It's my brother who's the technical man. He developed them, so I don't have all the technical info. All I know is it's good for the creatures and that's all I need to know. And for sure it is all *you* need to know. Now here, take this." He hands me a sort of riding crop thing. Only, it has a sharp nail end like the stick he wanted me to use on P-Hugh. Which I couldn't do. Which was why I got beat up and abused by the pink menace all day long. Still, I won't be able to use this one, either.

"So you want me to ride him," I say.

"No, I want you to piggyback him all over the property. Of course I want you to ride him!"

"I've never ridden a horse before."

"He's a *pony*! Now get in the saddle, follow that trail out that way, all the way out to the orchard. Give him a good workout and don't let him come back till he is good and tired out. He's a lazy, fat son of a gun, and he knows the trails, so he'll try and shortchange ya."

Mercury looks my way and paws the ground. That lazy fat remark just might cost me.

"And don't be chicken with that slapstick. He's a cuss, that pony is. He would use it on you if he had the slightest chance, so don't be shy."

"He's right about that," Mercury says to me. "In a heartbeat, I'd slapstick you silly if I could figure a way."

Bucky marches off to be mean and insane to some of earth's other unlucky creatures, and I attempt to start a friendship with Mercury. I approach the saddle area.

"You know, most animals really like me," I say.

"Show me one," Mercury says.

"Well, not around here. But honest, I'm famous in animal circles."

"Animal idiot circles, you mean."

"I didn't mean that, actually," I say, having had just about enough of this already. I see him angle his head toward me as I attempt the saddle thing. I hold the slapstick in what I hope is an intimidating fashion even though I wouldn't use it even if he pulled a gun on me. "Now, let's just try to make the best of this and get along, hmm?" I give the slapstick a little slap in my palm.

Before I know it, the vicious little pony has turned, snapped, and whipped the stick right out of my hand.

"Hey!" I say.

I can hear the whistle of wind as Mercury smacks me with the slapstick right across the thigh. Fortunately the nail end doesn't catch me, but just the same . . .

"Yeoww!" I shout, quickly wrestling the thing back out of the pony's teeth.

"Hey, hey," Mercury says, his mood much improved. "I did it."

"I'm very happy for you," I say, and jump right up on his back and take command.

Not knowing at all what I am doing kind of undermines my command, however. He takes off, and I can barely stay on.

"Slow down, Mercury," I say.

"No," he says. "I'm out of shape, remember? I need the work."

"I think you look fine. It's kind of sweet. Full-figured, is what I'd —"

He breaks into something faster. Canter? Gallop?

Bounce. He breaks into a bounce. I don't know if this is standard for ponies, but Mercury's spine doesn't seem to bend much when he goes, so the action is just like on a rocking horse, front-back, front-back, up-down, up-down.

I believe I somehow manage to look even more foolish than when I was locked in the weigh crate and got paraded around for the amusement of all. I am desperately clinging to Mercury's neck, attempting to hug him as hard as possible and thereby avoid crashing to the ground. As I squeeze, I am up close to the collar around his neck. I definitely hear a humming coming off it. And as my cheek brushes it, I get a shock. A sting. Then another. It's not regular, but random, irregular, and sharp.

"Please," I say. "Please go easy."

"Why should I?"

"Because I am your friend."

"No, you're not. None of you are our friends. We can tell as soon as we sense the chip, or a chip reader, or a scanner or whatever. You are one of them."

"But I'm not. I'm one of you. I'm here as a penalty, I'm a rehab project, just like they tell me you are."

Mercury does not slow down. He does his rocking horse thing just as bumpily and uncontrollably as before, and I'm on the verge of falling off him at any second.

Until suddenly I'm not on the verge. I am over the side, and hanging on to the saddle while my legs drag in the dirt and I plead to be released.

"No," Mercury says, and while I might think he would calm down, having already defeated me pretty definitively, he only seems to be getting angrier, snorting louder, running faster.

It feels like we have been running for hours by the time he slows down even a little. I consider just letting go now and hitting the ground, but that turns out to not even be possible, since my right hand is actually trapped, painfully twisted underneath the saddle.

But he does, finally and mercifully, come to a stop.

Okay, not mercifully.

"Please, Mercury, I can't breathe."

We are apparently at the orchard. I sense this because there is the whiff of apple in the air, mixed with pony sweat and terror as I lay pinned between Mercury's side and what I am guessing is an apple tree at my back.

"You never know when to stop," comes a molasses voice from somewhere beneath us. I manage to cock an eye downward to see a thick and serious reptilian somebody down there. He is addressing Mercury. "You probably made your point a while ago, and now you just can't help yourself. Am I right?"

"You're right," I say through a mouthful of pony shoulder. "You are so right."

"I'm just so *angry*," Mercury says, and manages to stomp the ground without either releasing me or squashing my head into sauce.

"Why? What did he do? Did he hit you with the slapstick?" The reptile turns to me. "You didn't hit him with the slapstick, did you?"

"No, I did not hit him with the slapstick. I don't even know where it is anymore. I lost it way back there someplace. We'll have to look for it on the way . . . owww! Owww. My head! Never mind — we don't need to find the slapstick."

And like that, the pressure reverses, and I am released

to gravity. I wriggle my hand out of the saddle and collapse like a sack of apples to the ground.

"So what did he do, Mercury?" the thick lizard asks.

"I don't know," Mercury answers. "But something. Feels like he did something. He needs a kicking. I hate him. And smell his breath. I smell beef on his breath. I can't wait till the bulls get ahold of him. Heh. Heh heh heh."

That *heh heh* stuff at the end gives me a chill. I lie there on my back, looking up into the apple trees and smelling them, trying to become almost serene.

There is a stout lizard on my chest now. His round, speckly yellow and black head is right up close to my face.

"Hi," I say.

"You *do* have hash breath."

"That's all they give me," I say.

He stands there staring, contemplating me. Lizards are great at that. Seems like they can stare and take it in for hours; you would never have a prayer of outlasting a lizard in a staring contest. But I have to risk rudeness and disturb whatever it is he's doing, because I'm a bit concerned.

"Sorry," I say as calmly as I can, "but are you a Gila monster?"

"I am *not* a monster," he says, and looks away. "I hate that. I really do."

"Sorry," I say. "I didn't mean anything by it."

"Apology accepted," he says, turning back to me.

"But you *are* highly poisonous, yes?"

If venom can be on their breath — and why couldn't it be? — then I am breathing it in right now.

"Yes," he says. "Not as bad as him, though."

He looks off to his left, I look off to my right, and we both settle there on the sight.

The sight rattles its tail at me. "Welcome," says the rattlesnake, his mouth open wide.

I used to know which venomous creature was which. Whether the tarantula paralyzed you and the scorpion gave you hallucinations . . . but I have to admit that I haven't kept up. So I don't know for certain whether the amount of juice in the vicinity is enough to paralyze me just by suggestion, but I do know I am paralyzed.

"I think you should breathe," says the Gila who is not a monster.

"If you say so," I reply. "That is, if you want me to."

"Why wouldn't I?"

"I don't know. Because the pony and the pig want to see me stop breathing, and that's even before the bulls get ahold of me. I have never been in a less friendly gathering in all my life."

The Gila climbs down off me and stands calmly next to the snake. I sit up, and the pony drifts among fallen apples, hopefully filling his belly with goodness.

"Nobody knows why those guys up there are that way. Must be the ranch work. Really seems to get them worked up. But when you ask them what the problem is, they never seem to know. Word is that they are all damaged already when they get there, and that's why they're there. I think maybe the damage happens at the ranch."

"Hey! Are you talking about me over there?" Mercury shouts, shooting apple bits like shrapnel across the way.

"No," says Gila calmly.

"You aren't like that, though," I say. "Even though you're obviously chipped. Is it because you got away?"

"No idea. I guess. But even when I was up there, I was never driven as wild as those big beasts."

He is very serene. He is making me feel better. Making me feel less scared and confused, even if I don't know what's happening.

"You're right — you are nothing like a monster. You're a Nonster."

Either a smile comes over him, or I'm about to sample the old venom. "I like that," he says. "You just made yourself a very toxic friend, sir."

"Well, I seem to have a gift for that."

Gizzard™ starts buzzing, then I hear the voice of Dr. Gristle.

"Speaking of . . ." I say.

"Zane!" Dr. Gristle explodes. "Where are you? Is it true you have escaped with one of my brother's prized specimens?"

The two potent reptiles in front of me scatter at the sound of the reptile on the screen.

"Escaped? What do you mean, escaped? I took the stupid pony for a ride like he told me to. Or, the pony took me . . . hey, wait, Bucky finked on me? He called you to squeal? How lame is that?"

"Don't pick on my brother. He is a simple, beautiful creature who just happens to get flustered when he has to think things through. He doesn't get along with technology, so I handle that end of things. And we *like* it this way, so don't interfere."

I feel the warmth of complication rising in my chest. This might be a good day after all.

"Interfere? Why would I —?"

"Because that's your thing, isn't it? It's what you do. Well, you aren't doing it now. Get back on that pony and head up to the ranch before my brother gets any more worried than he already is."

"Wouldn't want to worry Bucky," I needle.

The doctor's voice goes very low and very cold. The screen even darkens a bit and the contrast goes funny. "No," he says. "You really wouldn't."

At this moment, I'm inclined to believe him.

I start walking in the direction Mercury headed. Nonster and the snake reappear like little scales of sunshine.

"You handle the wicked one pretty comfortably," Nonster says.

"Takes practice," I say. "Not for amateurs."

Snake gives us a shake.

"And what's your story, little pal?" I say to Snake, feeling some of my animal magic coming back to me.

"Bite me," he hisses.

"Oh," I say, recoiling. "He's one of the damaged ones."

"No," Nonster says, "he's a rattlesnake."

"Right."

Nonster takes me on a slow walk to look around for Mercury and to see the orchard area. The rattler opts to stay behind.

"This place has a feel," I say, opening my arms and hands wide, touching the moisture in the air, breathing in the green and sweet, so different from the dry ranch air.

"Haven," Nonster says. "It's where you go when you escape. If you're small enough to hide and get away with it."

"I'd like to live here," I say.

A bird of prey, something tawny with a wingspan as wide as mine, makes a swoop right down through the trees and close enough to blow my hair forward over my eyes.

I brush the hair away and watch him push three and four great flaps of his wings and off he is again. It is a rush that has me grinning daffily.

"Makes my heart race to be so close to that, huh, Nonster?"

I look down to find his substantial self wedged sideways half under a boulder.

"Makes my heart explode, actually," he tells me.

"Oh, yeah," I say, "I guess it would. He's gone, though, so we can move on."

We move on through the orchard, which opens up to a more random selection of fruitless trees. It's less shaded, more spacious, still cool and lush. It is not nearly as dense as the woods of the WildWood back home, but there is definitely a connection.

"There aren't a lot of creatures down here," I say to Nonster.

"A lot of nocturnals," he says. "Because of the heat. But there are more around than you know. Doesn't pay to advertise, if you know what I mean."

"Makes sense."

We come to an ending of some kind, where the wood converts itself out to meadow, but not before making one last great woody statement about the difference.

"Whoa," I say, stopping and looking up. And up, and up, and over, and up. "Is that a tree or a planet?"

"What?" Nonster says, not even bothering to look up. "This old thing?"

"What am I looking at, Nonster?" I ask.

"Well, Zane, if you are looking at that tree right there . . . it's a tree."

"Not like any tree I've ever seen."

"Or, maybe like every tree you've ever seen?" comes a voice from dead ahead — a central dark opening, like a cave in the base of this massive, sprawling tree.

I walk toward it. "No, I think I was right the first time."

When I reach the tree-cave, a head pops out, followed by shoulders and arms. It's a kid — a couple of years older than me, I would say. He drapes himself over the lip of the cave, which is about six feet off the ground. He looks very confident, smiling down at me.

"If you're looking for that pony," the kid says, "he said to tell you he was heading back."

I flinch. He's joking, right? I should not jump to conclusions or give anything away. It's just an expression. He can't really understand the animals, because, well, he's not me.

"Right," I say. "The pony talked to you. Did he say anything else? Like what time to be home for supper?"

"No, but he did say he's bringing Bucky the slapstick, whatever that's supposed to mean. Is that some kind of code?"

Yikes, he *can* hear them.

Yikes, the slapstick.

"Okay, you," I say, going right up to the tree, stepping up and peering into the dark cave. I see more dark. "How can you hear what the pony says? How is that possible? Who do you know?"

The kid is laughing at me, at my insistence, at my pretending to have any kind of authority, here or anywhere else.

"I know you," he says.

"You do not."

"You're Zane."

"What? How do you know . . ." I am officially freaked out. From feeling like I have been removed from all the life I know back home — not entirely a bad thing — I suddenly feel like I've been thrown into an outback version of my electronic cage of a bedroom, which knows everything about me.

"Calm down. I heard little HavanaGila there call you that."

I look down. "That's your name? You could have just told me."

"I liked being reminded that I'm not a monster. Either way, I'm easy."

"Anyway," I say, back to the kid. "How, could you tell me, do you get to hear the animals?"

The kid looks down, HavanaGila looks up. They are conferring. I get the okay.

"It's the tree," the kid says with a broad smile. "I found it out by accident, being inside the Titanium Tree here, you can hear all kinds of stuff, coming from who knows where. It's like being inside a giant speaker that collects messages from outer space and inner animals."

I know my mouth is hanging open, because I feel a fruit fly take off from my tongue.

"Can I?" I ask, pointing beyond him into the opening.

"You don't even know my name yet," he says, scowling.

"Sorry," I say, holding out my hand for a hello shake.

"Edmund," he says, taking my hand and squeezing it so hard I expect to see the fingers bulge out like an inflated doctor's glove. "Gee, sorry there, Zane," he says, staring at my hand with pity and confusion. "But do you ever, like, *use* those hands?"

"Well," I say, "up till lately, the most strenuous thing they would do was wash each other. I would pretend they were wrestling, though . . ." I catch myself, a bit late. "But I am changing all that now."

"That's good. First change should be *don't tell anybody else that story.*"

Inside the cave, I am awed with the shock of the space. It seems like the inside of the tree is hollow, yet alive, and goes on forever. I smell the acid green of live wet wood, but also a distinct metallic tinge.

"You didn't tell me how *you* can hear the animals," Edmund says.

"I, oh . . . I'm a mutant," I say, ever clever.

"Well, that much I know — I felt those hands, remember? What's your job up at the ranch — milking butterflies?"

"Yes, I milk the butterflies, okay? And I *am* a mutant. I can't tell you more because I'm top secret."

"Fine," Edmund says. "My tree's better anyway."

"Not as portable," I point out. "You said it was a Titanium Tree?"

"Right. I heard that from an old owl."

"Of course."

"It's this crazy thing, like, petrified, calcified, from being thousands of years old. It's turned like a zingy metal but still alive at the same time." Edmund walks to a cave wall. "Here, taste."

I go right over and do as he does, putting my tongue to the surface.

Cold. Live, green, sap. And absolutely, clean metallic.

"It's kind of an everything tree," he continues. "There's no doubt some redwood in there, up there" — he points straight up — "some yew out there." He points out the opening to where the lower branches actually reach down into the earth and take root. "There's chestnut and oak and beech and all kinds of everything going on here crazy."

"I had a bagel like that before," I say, touching as much of the tree as I can reach from inside. "It was pretty great, but nothing like this."

"It wouldn't have tasted very good if it was made from magic millennia metal."

"No," I say, shaking my head, "it wouldn't. This is some special stuff, no doubt about it. I bet some people would be dying to get their hands on it."

"I would think so," Edmund says. "But tough, it's mine."

We are interrupted by an avalanche of sound, by a falling wall of shouting and bellowing and barking coming down from the ranch and entering the orchard.

"Bloodhounds," Edmund says.

I hear Bucky's whoopy little dog chatter — and the faint demented sound of the world's most unreasonably fierce pony — in my earpiece, and echoing around the hollow Titanium Tree, too.

"Party for you, I'm guessing," says Edmund.

"It's always a party for me," I say.

"They stopped looking for me a long time ago," he says, kind of sadly. "Almost before they started looking."

"You came from up there?" I ask.

"Yup. Fugitive from justice, like yourself."

"Well, I'm a fugitive from something, that's for sure. But it's definitely not justice."

"You want to hide?" he asks.

"No," I tell him, "I should go back." I swing a leg up over the lip of the cave and straddle it for a second. "I'll come back again, though. I'd like to meet up."

He waves me out, into the coming wave of love.

"I'm here a lot," he says, shaking my hand again, then shaking his head at the lameness of my grip.

"I'm working on it," I snap as he stares at his own hand like he's just pulled it out of cold pudding.

My punishment is swift and uncompromising.

"Dinner?" I ask from the back of a pony that is barely big enough for one.

"Dinner, sure," Bucky says from the front of that same pony. He did, after all, say Mercury needed the work.

"I'm going to kill you," Mercury says into my ear noodle.

"In the big house, with you and Mrs. Bucky?"

"That's right. We need to talk. And you could use a hearty meal by now, am I right?"

"About the need to talk, or the hearty meal?"

"Well, since I'm gonna talk at ya no matter what, let's say *meal*."

"Then you are absolutely right."

The pony trek back was weirdly serene — aside from the snarling pony, of course. I did hear the words *escape* and *retribution* and *punishment*, but they floated through the late afternoon air with such a Bucky-lite lilt, the badness wasn't apparent. I figured they were maybe words like *slaughter* and *bust* that cowpoke types seem to see as positive things.

The important thing is, I appear to be in a good place, at least for the time being. I have been invited up to the boss's for dinner, and even though I wrongly appear to have made a break for it today, my cage door is left open for me to make myself presentable on the honor system.

Starting with a nice, cold, open-air bath.

"Brrrr," I say to the setting sun. "Could you not set quite so quickly?" The air is still warm but things are changing rapidly, and the water temperature is already biting enough to make a guy think he can negotiate with the sun.

I nearly jump right out of my trough when a duck splashes down, over my shoulder into the water.

"Do you mind?" I say.

"Quack," he replies. I believe there is no chip — as well as no respect — in this duck.

On the subject of no respect, Pinkish Hugh ambles up. Without so much as a squeal, he dips his snout into my bathwater and starts drinking.

"Cut that out," I protest.

He is really gulping.

"Hey! You're going to have me naked to the world in a second."

He ignores me.

"Fine," I say, and take my homemade, Mrs. Bucky's Own brand Soap on a Rope — it's actually soap on a floppy willow stick — and plunge it in to soap up the water. Hah.

"Hah," I say when the pig's ugly pink head shows itself.

He stares at my stick soap, which I waggle triumphantly in his face.

Like a gator, he snaps the square chunky bar right off the willow and starts munching.

"Uk," I say.

"It's made from duck and goose fat." He slobbers.

Though the duck does not appear chipped, he does appear amused. *Wak-wak-wak* sounds very much like mockery right now. I lunge for him.

"I'll wash with *you* then," I say, just managing to snag a few feathers before his liftoff.

I am sitting, naked and freezing in half a tub of water, with the coward sun fleeing down past the horizon, when I am suddenly and completely surrounded.

Very much like a Christmas manger scene.

Only not.

"Hello," I say to the assembled party while hiding myself behind my willow stick. "I don't believe we've met."

"I don't believe we give an udder," says a voice within a big shaggy reddish head. There is a tongue visible, and a mighty metal nose ring, long bangs covering the whole rest of the face. A Highland bull. Oh, and horns growing as long as my arms out of each angry temple region.

"Do I detect a bit of a Scottish burr there?" I ask, my entire person shaking, the difference between fright and freezing becoming irrelevant.

"We want to tell you what we are going to do to you."

Oh, my word. I start shaking so tremendously, it's like I'm playing with a fleet of tiny nuclear subs in the bath.

"Can't you just do it to me, and let it be a surprise?"

"We know who you are," says a Clydesdale horse the size of a fire engine.

"I'm not him, I swear."

"Yes you are," says a black bull whose shoulders rise like the Matterhorn from behind his head. Each of these hulking beasts wears the same necklace of brick-size teeth. Each wears the same bloodred eyes.

"Listen, guys," I say, splashing myself quickly all over, "I have a dinner date."

"You have a date with us tomorrow," says the Highlander. "So enjoy your dinner with the boss tonight. Because you are not getting away with anything with us."

"Anything what? I'm not trying . . . why do you think . . . ?"

"We're not stupid," says the Clydesdale. "You come in here with the chip in you, you're working for them."

"That's not true," I plead. "Not true at all. I was sent here because I keep *ruining* Dr. Gristle's plans, not helping him."

"Hey!" comes the shout of a woman's voice — Mrs. Bucky, I presume. I turn to see her flying down from the big house in our direction, waving what looks like a broomstick. "How did you filthy beasts get out? Go on, get back, leave this boy alone."

The filthy beasts stand firm, even snorting and pawing at the ground. Which I think is a little lame, for three tons of muscle to be shoeing tough at one little lady.

Until she gets close and I see that the broomstick is more of a thin, long pitchfork, with sparkling, blinking pointed ends.

"Get away from him," she says, flying right into the black bull.

He leaps straight up, all four hooves off the ground. In midair he twists his body around so he lands facing the opposite direction and runs toward the paddock. Actually, he doesn't run so much as jump, bucking and kicking insanely at the air all the way.

The Clydesdale backs away without a fight and heads to his pen, but the Highlander squares and faces her.

Mrs. Bucky doesn't even flinch. She goes right into him

and jabs him on the snout with the fork. He lets out a bellow, halfway between an elephant's call and a trucker's air horn.

And when she stabs him again, in the foreleg, I hear something else. A *tzitz*. A crackle, a sizzle, like an electrical charge being set off.

Highlander goes mad. He bucks and swirls and looks to be trying to stab himself with his own horns on both sides, because he cannot get at the creature he really wants to skewer. Mrs. Bucky stands there poised for more trouble, until Highlander finally bucks off, howling with rage.

"Nice working with them, huh?" she calls back to me. "Dead meat, boy. Dead meat."

I have never ever seen that much pure fury in my whole life.

"Now," Mrs. Bucky says brightly, as if she'd just finished off a nice flower arrangement rather than terrorized the devil's own plow team. "You had better get yourself dressed, young man, because dinner is nearly ready. I wouldn't advise being late to one of Bucky's dinner invitations."

That sounds enough like a threat to pop me right up out of the bath.

Oh, right, the nakedness. You forget these things, under such circumstances.

"Oh, dear," Mrs. Bucky says, swinging herself back toward her dinner preparations.

"Bwooiiink!" says the hysterically laughing pig rolling in the dirt a few yards away. "And they call *me* pinkish!"

———•———

I am right on time for dinner, and am shown right to my seat. The dining room is a modest place, with a big rough oak table and chairs for eight people. There are animal heads mounted just below ceiling height all the way around the room. Wolf, fox, beaver, otter, deer, puma, brown bear, horned owl, alligator, coyote, hare, Rocky Mountain bighorn sheep, and hammerhead shark all look down on us, giving their blessings to the bounty we are about to receive.

"You sure do love animals, Bucky," I say, needing to take my wise-guy muscles out for a stroll.

"Yes, I surely do," he says, looking lovingly up at the crowd.

Mrs. Bucky sets down three bowls of soup for us. "Thank you, Mrs. Bucky," I say.

"Please," she says, "it's Becky."

"Thank you, Becky Bucky," I say, sipping my soup. I should have waited, since the soup is so hot I have no idea what flavor it is. "Ow."

"Not Becky Bucky, son. Becky Gristle. But just Becky is fine."

"How do ya think you're getting on?" asks Bucky bluntly. He dives right into his soup, and then dives again. "Oh, the best, Becks," he says.

"Thank you," she says, sipping at hers.

I try it again. "Ow."

"I think I am getting on . . . okay, sir," I say. "It's hard work, no doubt about that. And you sure do have a collection of spirited animals."

The two of them burst out laughing. "Oh, yes," Bucky says. "We are renowned for that. We get all your problem children here, human and beast kind alike. But through a program of good hard work, healthy living, and loving discipline, we feel like we can get every last one to become a useful contributor to the good of the world. Even you."

They have both finished their soup, and Becky gets up to remove the bowls. I desperately try to catch up. "Ow," I say, through the spoonful. Then I take another and another before I allow her to have mine.

Their mouths must be flame retardant. And I still don't know what kind of soup it was.

"I bet you're wondering why I would invite you up here," Bucky says when we're alone.

"A little, yes."

"Well, for starters I thought I'd fill you in a little bit on what to expect in the coming days. First off, you can expect some painful buttocks tomorrow morning."

"What? No, I'm fine."

"Right. When was the last time you were on a pony?"

"Um, let me think . . . oh, never."

"Right. Tomorrow morning you'll see what I mean.

Then you'll start feeling a lot of other aches and pains and stresses and strains, as we put you through some paces I suspect you have never been through before."

"I suspect your suspicion is correct," I say.

"Good. Well, tomorrow you have a special treat."

"I do?"

"Yes indeed. Couple times a year, we have a good friend, a one-of-a-kind kinda talent, who passes through these parts. He's known as the Conquistador, and he's a bullfighter."

I feel my whole face bulge into the frozen expressions I see up on the wall.

"A *bullfighter*? Do people still do that?"

"Special people do, yes. And one of the finest will be here tomorrow, to put on an exhibition, and to give our animals a workout. It will be magnificent, and you are lucky to be here for it."

I'm still startled. "*Those* bulls? The ones I . . . met? Those gigantic carvings of muscle and hatred? He's going to fight them?"

"Yes, sir."

"What's he going to fight them with — an aircraft carrier?"

"With this," Bucky says, tapping his temple with his middle finger.

"I don't mean to be negative, Bucky, but I think anybody who fights *them*" — I point out the window toward the fields — "with *this*" — I tap my own coconut — "is going to find *this*" — coconut again — "up *there*" — I point to the spot on the wall between badger and buzzard heads.

Bucky lets out a roar, and Becky joins him, though I think she is just being supportive since she walks in a tad late to have heard.

"You will see, my friend," Bucky promises.

Becky lays down a platter of what is instantly the most wooz-inducing main dish I have ever smelled. She can see that I'm caught in its spell because she grins proudly and fills me in.

"It's called five-bird roast, Zane. It is the boned breast of a quail, inside a pigeon, inside a chicken, inside a duck, inside a turkey. Sometimes you can use goose, but . . ."

"And it is all mummified inside a complete blanket of bacon," I say, "more mummified than the birds."

"Correct, and then slowly roasted together until practically melting."

I apologize to all my bird friends in the world. I am sure that on some level I feel terrible about what I am about to do, but I am equally sure I am going to do it until I get sick, and then possibly do it some more.

It clearly does Becky's poultry-menacing heart good to begin carving into this creation, as she does so humming a tune. I think it's "Candy Man."

"And you know who else is going to have the honor of seeing the show for himself?" Bucky says.

I sense a little parade rain here.

"Who?"

"Your good friend and mentor, my brother, Dr. Gary Gristle."

I allow myself a blurting. "Mentor?" I blurt. "You did mean to say 'mental,' right? He's not my good friend or anything like that. He keeps putting me in places like this."

"Oh, now, Zane, there is no place like this, to be fair. And besides, have you not yet recognized that the things my brother keeps doing are all designed for your own improvement? He sees great potential in you, I'll have you know."

"Potential to mess up his demented plans, you mean."

"My goodness, you *are* feisty," Bucky says in a not-unfriendly tone. "Isn't he feisty, Becky?"

"Feisty," Becky chirps, carving, humming. It's definitely "Candy Man."

"Feisty," Bucky says again. "Just like one of our fire-breathing bulls here. Maybe the Conquistador should fight *you* tomorrow."

"I can't fight him. I left my gloves at home."

"Oh, that's okay. We'll find you a job. Funny you should mention home, though."

Becky comes around and places gloriously upholstered plates of food in front of us. Thick sections of the multiplex bird, honey-glazed roasted sweet potatoes, and giant green beans shiny with butter and slivered almonds.

"Sorry," I say through the dazzle of glory and starvation. "What was funny?"

"That you should mention home. How would you like to go home with Dr. Gristle tomorrow?"

"Yeeek!" That involuntary scream comes out of me again, sounding like the birds have come back to life and seen themselves like this.

"I don't mean to his home, Zane. I mean your home. You could go back when the doctor goes back. And avoid what I think you now see is a pretty grueling time coming up here for you."

"Okay," I say, refraining from touching silverware until this is out. "How does that work?"

"Just tell me your secret, and I can set you free."

He lays that horrible family grin on me and I cover my mouth to stifle yet another scream. Then I pull it together, act calm, and tell my host politely, "I have nothing to tell you. Whatever it is your brother thinks he's after, I can't help you with it. I'm sorry."

How things do change in a hurry.

Quicker than if they sprouted their wings again, all those birds fly right off the table before my eyes. Becky sweeps my meal away at Bucky's barked command of "Dinner Plan B!" He gets up with his plate and storms off. "I'm eating in the bedroom," he says. "Get a good rest tonight, Zane, because you're going to need it."

I do wish he'd stop saying that.

Becky takes my plate to the kitchen and returns to find me sitting like a dodo, stunned into nothingness. With a sympathetic smile she presents Dinner Plan B.

Liquidy hash and beans. On my tin plate. With my unhelpful fork.

She takes the serving platter out of harm's way, disappearing again into the kitchen. A minute later she rushes back in. She quickly dumps several sweet potatoes onto my plate, looking over her shoulder nervously after. Then she looks back to me sadly.

"I did see you hop up out of that bath. Poor thing. Eat, eat."

And with one more Buck Bark from the other room, she is gone, taking her plate with her.

I sit there in the dining room and eat my food quietly, in the company of all the other dumb, doomed trophy heads.

The sweet potatoes are amazing and make me want to cry.

FIGHTING BULL

"Fuze, could you just, like, not bother me this morning. I have a lot going on here. And why haven't my parents contacted me?"

"Your mother said to tell you she's sorry, but there's been a lot of news lately."

"Oh, that's okay, then. Tell my mother I understand. We wouldn't want her tied up with her tortured and abused son while the 'news' happened without her."

"I'll tell her."

"How is Hugo No-Go? How's he doing?"

"Hugo Go-Go now. I have him right as rain."

"Zane," Hugo calls from somewhere, but I can't see him. "Zane, you have to help me. It's torture here. Worse than where you are."

"Fuze, where is Hugo? I want to see him."

"Why? Don't you trust me?"

"No, I don't. Stay out of my room. Where is my

dog? Tell my father I want to hear from him. Show me my dog."

"Oh, your dog has been telling me all about you, Zane, you little devil."

"He's been telling . . . ? Hugo! Hugo, where are you? Hugo, what have you done?"

"Jeepers," Fuze says, "have they broken you already? You sound nuts, frankly. Of course the dog hasn't been talking to me. Exactly how crazy are you, Zane?"

"Very. I want to see my dog, Fuze. Put Hugo to the camera right now."

With a giggle, Fuze reaches off camera and comes back with a version of Hugo in her arms.

"Bwaaa," I laugh out loud, and am instantly aware how good that feels right now.

Hugo is dressed in a great big baby bonnet to cover his great big head. He's also wearing a diaper.

"I am going to kill you," Hugo says.

"Yeah, well, you'll have to take a number," I say.

"A number for what?" Fuze says.

"Sorry, just thinking out loud."

"Well, think about this. If you don't do something about this humiliation I'm suffering every day, I might accidentally lead Fuze on a tour of all your secret places that only your dog —"

"Fuze, take that stupid hat off him right now."

"I don't think I like your tone," she says.

Hugo, slouched in her lap, looks a lot like a baby. Now she starts doing this thing, flicking up his front paws like he's doing a sweet little hand dance.

"Change your *tone*, Zane," he says.

"I would really appreciate it, Fuze, if —"

"Call me Lori."

"I would appreciate it, Lori —"

"Lorilai," she says.

"Please, if you don't mind, Lorilai . . ."

Satisfied, she undoes the bow at his chin, and he starts panting as if he has just been released from some scorching sweatbox of a cage.

"Now the diaper," he says.

"And the diaper, please?"

"Sorry," she says, "I didn't quite hear . . ."

"Lorilai!" Hugo shouts at me.

"The diaper, please, Lorilai?"

"Sorry, but the diaper is for medical purposes. It was prescribed by Hugo's personal physician."

"Dr. Gristle? You saw Dr. Gristle?"

"Well, yes, of course. With all of the intestinal trouble Hugo has been having, I had to make sure he was seen to. Your father made an appointment and sent us to the doctor. And I have to say, what a lovely man. He has got the sweetest, most heartwarming smile."

"Help me!" Hugo says. "I'm begging."

He's actually doing that two-paws-up begging maneuver that regular dogs do but it is horrifically unnatural to him.

"Fuze, I need you to do something. Dr. Gristle is coming up here today. I want you to bring Hugo to him. I want you to tell him that my father insists that I have a visit from my dog, for my mental health."

"Did your father say that?"

"He talks about my mental health a lot. He had to have said that at some point, I'm certain. Now, go. This is very important."

"Well, okay. But it sounds like you owe me one."

"One what?"

"I don't know, but whatever one people are talking about when they say, 'you owe me one.'"

"Fine, I'll owe you one of those. Just get Hugo to Gristle's."

"He wears nice clothes, too, the doctor. He wears shoes that you can really trust."

"Go!"

As soon as they've signed off and I have my cage to myself again, I go back to fretting. More than at any other time since I started interacting with the animals, I feel like I'm in real danger. I mean, Gristle is certainly dangerous, and usually all too happy to demonstrate that, but he's the devil I know. I always feel like one way or another I can handle him.

But the animals. The animals and I have always been on the same team. I have never felt threatened by the animals in any substantial way.

Now, I feel the threat. And it's substantial.

I cannot let this be. I must try to do something to bring them on my side.

I don't know if it's a special treat in a last-meal kind of a way, or just that he cannot stand to see me now, but Bucky leaves me alone with my breakfast, which happens to be a delightfully surprising platter of hash and beans. I know I'm going to need it, so I do eat every bit, and the fact that he doesn't have the stopwatch on me actually makes the food taste like less disagreeable slop.

I am also allowed to let myself out, and I rise from my slab with some effort. Ouch. Ouch.

Bucky appears to have been right on the money about the buttock discomfort. I guess there are some things he's just an authority on, ol' Buck.

Ouch. Ouch.

So this is why cowboys always walk this way.

I guess you could say I go out looking for trouble. It's not that I'm brave or anything, because with every wobbly step I can feel my knees offering themselves to the ground so I can beg whoever for forgiveness and mercy. But I have to at least try to do this. If I can get at least one of the big beasts to see the reality, to understand the absurdity of thinking of me as the enemy, I will at least have taken the first step to getting something achieved here.

Then who knows what we can accomplish?

I'm sweating already as I reach the yard. When I get there, I find nothing and nobody. So I push on, into what is already the hottest sunshine I have encountered yet. I walk over to my bathtub/drinking fountain/community center, and dunk my head right under. I take a short drink and set off, dripping, toward the fields.

There is no real water around the place, I notice. Not anywhere around. No river, no stream. It adds to the cracked, parched feeling of everything from the fence posts to the pale brown ground to the air.

I reach the first paddock, just up the rise toward the grazing fields, and find nothing. I continue up the hillock to where the Clydesdale was yesterday, having the field to himself. It's Clydeless. I reach the top of the small bump of a hill and turn around to take in my immediate past.

Ghostly. It's like a little tumbleweed town because there's no sign of any life-form I recognize. There are no big beasts, no smaller beasts, no sheep or goats or pigs. There are no chickens or ducks or even any flyby birds stopping for a refueling. There are no bees, as far as I can tell.

In the middle of the intensity of the heat, I get a small chill. And I leave.

I make the long walk down the road I took with the pony. The ponyless pony trek toward the orchard. Every step is hotter than the last one and I keep looking over my shoulder to see how far I've gone. The stubborn ranch, just sitting there hardly moving, makes it feel like I am treading hard to nowhere, so I push on and I stop checking.

Mercury must have dragged and bounced me along at a much greater pace than I thought, because this little trip is not any kind of little today. The sun of course makes it seem worse, and my feet are now hurting in a way that challenges my buttocks, but there's no denying there's a healthy bit of road between the ranch and the orchard.

Or an unhealthy bit of road. By the time I struggle into the first bit of shade provided by those welcoming fruit trees, I am very close to taking an involuntary seat on the ground. Instead, I grab at the first, lowest, mostly green apple I can get my mitts on, and I bite.

My eyes pull tight shut with the sourness of this apple, but I am not deterred. I hang on to it, sucking out the moisture and coolness and whatever level of energy and nutrition it is willing to provide me.

And I feel improved already. Not a ton improved, but functional.

So I function. And I function a little further, and then

a little further. It is as if the orchard itself, with its outstanding air and leafy-lifeyness, has the ability to pump a body back into shape just by passing through.

And before I can think about getting tired again, I have functioned my way all the way to the Titanium Tree.

I go right up, grab the lip of the big opening, and start to hoist myself up.

"Don't you even knock?" Edmund says, leaning right in my face.

I lose my grip and fall straight back down to the ground. I lie there staring up at him. He stares right back.

"Knock, knock," I say.

"Who's there?" he says.

"It's not a knock-knock joke."

"It's not a knock-knock joke, who?"

"It's not a knock-knock joke, shut up."

"Okay then, come on up."

It turns out, you don't actually have to climb this tree. Not the way you climb most trees, anyway. It's more like the way you would climb a mountain, almost walking up, but using your hands as well as your feet. There are trails leading you around and around and up, from one branch to the next, from one level to the next. It really is a world to itself, and I have to be careful as I follow along behind Edmund that I don't stare off and up in wonder and lose my footing.

"So, are you here, like, all the time?" I ask him.

"Like," he says.

"Where are you the other times, then?"

"Elsewhere."

"Oh."

The tree, as he told me, has got it all. It is both leafy and piney, with needles that smell strong and pinch with authority. There are random twisty branches that burst open at the tips with leaves that look like silvery little hands or starfish. There is a thick and shiny arrangement of ivy that absolutely swarms over much of the trunk, and other bare patches that expose the least barky bark I have ever seen. It is part flakes of metallic skin, part rubber, paper, shiny fish scales.

I have nearly traveled as far vertically as I have horizontally today.

"There were no animals when I got up today," I tell him.

"It happens," he says casually.

"Why does it happen?"

"I never had a chance to find out. The big ones, I think they get taken aside somewhere, for some secret goings-on. The rest of them, they just go into hiding. No idea what that's about."

"Why are there no animals here?" I ask as we come within sight of the top.

"What do you mean? It's loaded with animals here. You just need to know how to look."

Edmund has a satisfied mischievous look on his face as he waits on a fat branch for me to catch up. Like he's been waiting for me to ask this.

When I get there, he leans in and parts a couple of great bunches of soft ivy, like curtains.

"Hey," says a possum hanging there.

"Hey," I say.

It's a remarkably perfect miniature of the big cave at the bottom. We go along now and every few feet Edmund parts the ivy curtains to reveal another cubbyhole and another inhabitant or three. Hello, raccoon. Hello, woodpecker family.

"It's like a massive animal apartment building," I say.

"Exactly," Edmund says. "That's how they can just hide forever and not be noticed. The less notice we get down here, the better. There's something that sets them off and they all go into hiding, like every two weeks. Like when a storm is coming and the animals seem to know it? I haven't figured out what it is, but maybe it has something to do with your disappearing animal trick up there at the ranch."

"Maybe it does," I say, but I'm already distracted by what's ahead. It's the peak. The opening at the top of the tree, at the top of the world.

"Oh, my," I say as we break through. "Oh, my, my."

The top of the tree opens up into what can best be described as an eagle's nest. For human-size eagles. There is a central hole that we climb through, and then we are in the center of a tightly woven, willowlike construction of nest that must be fifteen feet in diameter. I could bring my bed up here.

I keep rubbing my eyes. I look in all directions, and the sun is even more unforgiving, but I keep staring and I keep rubbing my eyes, which I don't want to do, because when I rub, I can't see this.

Edmund is laughing silly, because he just knows. He probably dies to show this to people, since I know I would.

Not even in my dreams. Not even in my dreams when I was flying. I was never this high and never thought about this high. I never dreamed that there was such a thing as this high.

"Nice, isn't it?" Edmund says. "You can see practically the whole world from up here, while no one can see you."

"It's true. I can see the ranch, like I'm looking through a telescope. Like it's right there and I can reach out and touch it."

In a second I feel Edmund's hands on me, holding me at the ribs. I look down at his hands to see that I am, in fact, leaning into the sight, the vision in the distance.

"You have to be careful about that," he says. "Falling off would spoil the view, I think."

"I think," I say. "Thanks."

I return to the view and, I realize, the sound. As clear as the vision is of every detail of the ranch, the sounds, all the sounds, are coming across as clearly as Hugo speaking through the Gizzard™ and into my ear noodle. Only the Gizzard™ and noodle have nothing to do with it.

"I know," Edmund says when he sees my face. "It's great if you like to eavesdrop." He walks to the center of the nest, where spikes of tip-top branches of the Titanium Tree shoot up. He pings one, and the sound gets louder, but crackly. Then it settles down again. "It's the tree that sees all, hears all, knows all," he says.

I turn back to the scene at the Primeval Ranch. All the animals are there, doing their thing as if they were never gone. Were they never gone? Maybe I just passed through one more illusion; it seems to be happening all the time. Maybe it's even happening to me now. Maybe I'm not seeing them at all. Maybe heat and stress and fear are all getting to me.

"What happens to you when a Gila monster bites you?" I ask.

A small voice rises up on thin air. "I am *not* a monster."

"You don't really think HavanaGila bit you, do you?" Edmund asks.

"No," I say, "I guess not. But there seems to be a lot going on in my head, and I can't make sense of it all."

"Then you're probably right," Edmund says. "My experience has been generally, and especially around here, that if you think you're making sense of everything, you're probably losing it altogether."

I look at him for confirmation in his wide, bright features. He appears to mean it.

"Okay," I say, looking back. "I'll keep that in mind. But right now, I do think I need to be making my way back down. It seems like we've got a full house already at the ranch. Want to see a bullfight?"

"No, sirree. I saw that when I was there the first time, and I never, ever want to see the likes of it again. You have a nice time, though."

"Well, I don't expect to, and . . . oh, puke. What is this? What has he gone and brought Fuze here for? I have to go. Rats. Puke."

"Ratspuke to you, too, my friend. Is that like *vaya con dios?*"

BULLTEASING

I am almost crawling by the time I swing back through the corral gate.

"Where on earth have you been, young man?"

That line is spoken simultaneously by a crazy rancher in chaps, his veterinarian-scarian brother, the girl who is living my life while the position is vacant, and a white mutt terrier in a diaper.

If it sounds like any of them are concerned for my welfare, that is merely an illusion.

Less illusional is the greeting I get from elsewhere.

"Dead meat. You may be moving, but you aren't fooling anybody. You are dead."

That's the black bull, Bistro. The Highlander just keeps running headlong into the fence post, too enraged to even threaten me. Clyde is galloping around his paddock in a way I don't think Clydesdales are meant to.

"It's nice to be missed," I say to the concerned parties.

Hugo comes barreling up to me with great enthusiasm, like I've been washing myself in goose fat.

And I fall for it. That's what a weakened state I'm in.

"Oh, buddy-buddy," I say, gathering him up and squeezing him tight. It's a great feeling.

For three seconds. He starts kicking and clawing to stop my gush.

"Get it off, get it off, Zane. Get this stupid thing off me right this second. It's even worse since I've been here in tough guy outdoorsyland. A gang of blue bloodhounds surrounded me and threatened unspeakable things until they howled so hard with laughter they couldn't speak, any of them. A duck said he was going to give me a wedgie. Zane, a *duck*!"

What kind of a guy lets his dog get a wedgie from a duck?

I tear the diaper off him (luckily, it's empty) and he jumps to the ground. He runs in circles crying out, "Freedom! Freedom!"

Next thing I know, the Brothers Griz are standing in front of me, uncomfortably close, arms folded.

"Where have you been?" Bucky asks.

"Well, when I came out, there was nobody here. Even all the animals were gone. So I went looking for company. Where were all the animals?"

"I . . . took them for a walk," Bucky says.

"All of them?"

"Stop that, Bucky," Dr. Gristle interrupts. "See, I warned you, this is what he does. He turns things around so that . . . next thing you know you'll be answering all his questions, then where would we be?"

"Yes, where indeed?" comes the small crackly voice in my ear noodle.

"Huh?" I ask.

"Is this working? Zane, can you really hear me now?"

"Uh-huh," I say, trying to answer Edmund while seeming to cooperate with the prickly Gristlies.

"Whoa," Edmund says. "I'm up in the nest. Your signal was coming in so strong, so I just decided to talk into this here. It transmits, too. Wild."

"Wild."

"What is wild, Zane?" Dr. Gristle asks.

"Oh, the big animals. They seem even wilder and angrier than usual. And that is pretty wild."

"They're not wild," Bucky insists. "They are high-spirited. I think they have a sense somehow for when the Conquistador is here. It gets them very excited. They love a good honest fight."

"They do?"

I hear them smashing and thrashing in their pens. Bellowing, snorting.

"Yes," Dr. Gristle snaps. "They absolutely relish the fight. They are thrilled, and as their doctor, I would know."

I believe the bulls heard that, as they go wholly nuts now.

"As my doctor," the Highlander grunts, "I'd like you to know the sharp end of my horns."

"Hiya, Zane," Fuze says, stepping up between the men.

"Stay out of my room, Fuze," I say.

"Don't be rude," Dr. Gristle says to me while patting Fuze on the head. "Little Lori here has been very helpful in your absence. She is working with me to take the best care of your pet. She is even filling in from now on at my office, doing the job you did, before you went sour on me yet again."

"Ratspuke," I say in frustration.

"Don't be sour, Zane," she chides.

"Yes, your sourness is not helping you, and that is one of the things you are here to stamp out."

"My sourness levels are just fine, thanks," I say.

"Not according to your wall, Zany," Fuze says. "Your pH/alkaline balance is somewhere between lime rind and earwax."

"Stay out of my room, Fuze," I repeat.

"Bucky, don't you think it's time for Zane to get ready?" Dr. Gristle asks.

"Certainly is," Bucky says.

"Ready for what?" I ask.

"For your part," he says, stepping up and handing me a colorful flat box with a cellophane panel on the front. Inside is a clown costume.

"What is this?" I ask grimly.

"It's your special, custom rodeo outfit."

"There is nothing custom about it. It came from a joke shop."

"That's our custom," Dr. Gristle says, giggling at his latest funny. Fuze giggles along like a starstruck fan.

So does Hugo.

"How would you like that di-dee back there, Go-Go?" I snap at him.

Threatening my dog may make me look nuts and mean, but it does quiet him.

"Why am I supposed to wear this?" I ask.

"Every rodeo has to have a rodeo clown," Bucky says. "It's tradition."

"It's not even a rodeo. It's a bullfight."

"It can be both." He sounds defensive.

"Zane," Dr. Gristle says, "as part of your rehabilitation, you are not permitted to question the program set out for you."

"Program? There is no program, other than to humiliate and brutalize me until I'm broken."

Dr. Gristle turns and glares down at his little brother. "You told him."

"No, I swear, he just guessed."

"Well, you have to be the rodeo clown, Zane. So go back to your room and change."

"It's not a room, it's a cage," I protest.

"It's not a cage, it's a stable," Bucky insists.

I stomp off in the direction of the stables.

"See, I told you," Dr. Gristle says. "Absolutely ungrateful."

—◆—

"You're not really putting that thing on," Edmund says in my ear.

"I *am* putting it on, and I'm wearing it with pride," I say. The outfit is a rainbow-colored one-piece made of a hideously unnatural shiny material that is probably so flammable the sharp sunlight will set it on fire. And there is a matching wig. I slip the onesie up over my clothes and shove the wig down over my head. I have no mirror in my room. Terrible shame.

I nearly blind myself when I walk back out into the light.

My ear noodle is rocking with laughter, from high up in the Titanium Tree, and low, low down where my dog has come to lend me immoral support.

"It is only because we share some history that I don't give you the fire hydrant treatment right now," Hugo says.

"Thanks, pal," I say as I march with great dignity over to the big training pen that is usually used for working out the horses. It turns out that my job is not actually to be out there in the ring, but to keep up a presence on the side of the fence just in case the bullfighter gets himself into any difficulty. I'm the diversion.

I'm up and hanging over the top rail, on the opposite side of the ring from everybody else, when the Conquistador comes prancing along. He seems to be thinking that he's making some grand entrance, even though it's a pretty modest crowd and he left his suit of lights back at the tailor's or electrician's or wherever they leave them. His all-denim outfit does seem several sizes too small, though, so he's partway there.

The Conquistador exchanges pleasantries with the assembled crowd. He kisses Fuze's hand. When she responds by punching him hard in the shoulder, he is knocked back several steps and looks like he might cry.

At the far end of the ring, I see Becky driving the black bull toward the gate to enter the ring. He is clearly agitated, but every time he makes an unstraightforward move or even attempts to look in her direction, he gets a swift and firm jab with her devil fork, and he looks straight again, eyes ever redder, snorts ever snortier.

Then he's in the ring, and jogging, then bouncing, making harsh noises.

"Zane," Edmund says in my ear, "what is it about those collars the animals wear? The Gristles and that other guy keep mentioning them, but it keeps breaking up so I can't tell what it's about."

"I have no idea. It's another one of the doctor's experiments, I'm sure, but I can't tell what it is."

The bullfighter now enters the ring from the opposite side from Bistro.

I hear laughter. I turn to see Hugo staring up at me.

"Can I help you?" I ask.

"Shouldn't you have really big shoes on?"

"Shouldn't you have safety pantswear on?"

"I think this place is making you mean," he says. "I think I like new girl better."

I hear shouts of excitement and turn back to the real action, which has gotten hot already. Bistro is so enraged he is running crazy, almost aimlessly, as he tries to sink his horns into the Conquistador.

Conquistador swirls his cape, and Bistro misses wide. Bistro makes circles in the dirt when he rushes, then misses, then pivots, then rushes, then misses, then pivots again. The circles get tighter and tighter the more he misses. He is getting blind with rage now. The Conquistador carries a short, swordlike thing in his non-cape hand, like the slapstick I didn't use the other day. It's got a sort of nail in the end, and a stiff, firm shaft. Sometimes when the bull misses, he gives him a stylish jab with the nail. Sometimes, he actually takes the shaft and smacks Bistro on the snout or butt or, oddly, on the end of one horn or the other.

Each of these moves brings a howl of pain and anger out of Bistro, and at some point early in, I lose the ability to fear and dislike him.

It's so unfair.

And he hates it so much.

And it goes on and on.

I don't know how you could call this a fight of any kind. If you did it to a dog, they would call it teasing. Bullteasing would be a more accurate label for what is going on, but I suspect that would be embarrassing for both the Conquistador and the fans, and we don't want to embarrass them, so it remains bull*fighting* and the only one being humiliated is the bull.

"Come on, Bistro!" I suddenly, spontaneously cheer.

The Conquistador appears startled, maybe because nobody's ever cheered the bull before. He throws me a look.

Bistro seizes the day — or at least this tiny sweaty little bit of it — to run full-on into the Conquistador, catching him flush in the chest with the broad, flat middle of his head.

The bullfighter sails backward about ten feet before tumbling over. I remember my one real job, and start shouting, whistling, and shaking my multicolor head at the bull. He stops, turns my way, and instantly works out my clever disguise. While pretty low on energy at this point, he obviously still has a full tank of hate on board, because he summons enough speed to head madly in my direction like a muscular rocket.

He reaches my corner at full speed.

The impact of Bistro's head with my corner fence post is like getting hit in the head with a bat and thrown forward like a football. I travel right over him and land in a big cloud of dust on the other side of him.

Lucky for me he is disoriented now. He gets to his feet at the same time I do, and I continue to look at his back as he merely stares at the corner post.

"The barrel, Zane!" Bucky shouts. "The barrel!"

He's pointing to a wooden barrel in the next nearest corner of the ring. I run for it as fast as I can and hop in, just like a real rodeo clown would.

It's thickly padded all around the inside, and except for the fact it's about a hundred million degrees inside, it would be a comfortable place to spend some time.

But not this much time.

I'm waiting for ages, just about filling the whole barrel with sweat, but afraid to so much as peek out and find my head like a cocktail meatball on Bistro's horn. Then I do hear stirring, and voices a ways away, so I think I can risk it.

"Beautiful," Dr. Gristle says. "Off the charts."

The two Gristles and the Conquistador are busy working the big necklace off the big neck of the big Bistro. It comes off with some difficulty, as I see underneath it is actually connected deep into the bull's neck with tubes, wires, and probes.

"Great work, Conq," Bucky says, slapping Conquistador on the back.

The doctor finally gets the collar off as Bistro appears to get the beginnings of his wits back. "Hurry," Gristle says, as he and his brother work quickly to get a new collar back on, essentially nailing and threading it in place.

"Zane, nice work," Bucky says when he sees me cowering and peeking. "Now get back to your station for the next one."

The next one. Becky comes out and guides the exhausted bull back out of the ring, and this time he doesn't even express an interest in getting a look at her or killing anyone. He looks defeated and powerless.

"Oh, it'll take some time to get *those* levels back up," Dr. Gristle says jokily from the other side of the fence now. His assistant, the giant faceless space-suited government goon type he likes to have with him, appears out of nowhere to accept the bull's belt from him and take it away.

The Highlander is being directed into the ring now.

The Conquistador stands proudly, waiting, his chest puffed out, but not quite as puffed as before.

PIGS FLY

The second alleged bullfight runs along just about the same lines as the first one. Conquistador masterfully winds Highlander into such a fury he can't see straight. He twirls him and pokes him and slaps him into a rage that makes him just lunge pointlessly for three-quarters of an hour in the broiling sun. With all that red hair, I imagine Highlander is so overheated it's only pure undiluted anger keeping him on his feet.

Until he isn't on his feet anymore.

He drops to his knees and just huffs painfully for several minutes at the end, while the bullfighter prances and gloats two feet in front of him.

I had been openly rooting for Highlander throughout, with help from howling Hugo and even Fuze. Now I turn to booing and harassing him.

Eventually I hop down from the fence and get right into the action.

"I think he's thrown in the towel," I say, stepping between the two fighters. "What, are you waiting for him to empty his pockets? Get outta here."

Conquistador turns on his toes without a flicker of recognition that I'm even there. With his cape draped over one arm and his bullstabber raised high over his head, he acknowledges the cheers of a grateful fandom.

Both of them.

The brothers come rushing up to him, praising and thanking him. Bucky hands over a stack of cash. I turn away.

"I realize you hate me just like you hate them," I say to Highlander, "but I am genuinely sorry. Sorry for whatever they do to you here.

He offers me barely more recognition than Conquistador did, but who could blame him. He's got little stick jabs all over his back and shoulders, he can't lift his head off the ground from exhaustion. But at least he's not threatening my life.

I notice that even the tips of his horns seem red and irritated. I reach out and touch one — and he lets out a sort of scream-shout, but without lifting his head.

His horns appear to have been filed down. They look like giant fingers where the nails have been cut off way below the cuticle line. It hurts just to look at them, never mind jab them at someone. Or have somebody whack them with a stick.

"Excuse us there, rodeo clown," Bucky says as he and his brother kneel down and start working on Highlander. They are not working to make him more comfortable, of course, but to remove his collar.

It's even worse up close, with the doctor using a pair of needle-nose pliers to extract two stainless steel straws out of the underside of the neck, and several electrode things out of the top. All those lines feed in and out of the ceramic brick things that ring the necklace.

"What is all this stuff?" I demand of them.

"Sorry, my boy," Dr. Gristle says, "but you currently do not have the clearance to be included in the higher-level proprietary information related to the breathtaking advances of the Gristle techno-bio miracle."

"Huh?" Bucky says.

"Shush, Bucky," his brother says.

Becky shows up with her devil fork as they wrench the old collar off of Highlander and work the fresh and shiny one onto him. As the two bullcookies scurry away, pleased with their haul — even if Bucky's as clueless as me about the haul — Becky stands menacingly in front of Highlander, whistling and hooting at him to get up. She laps the devil fork into one palm with the other hand.

Highlander can see he's supposed to get up. But he's still not quite ready.

"Give him some time," I say.

"He's out of time," she says, and gives him a jolt on the shoulder.

"Come on, boy," I say. Regardless of the consequences from either side, I have to do something. I grab his two great horns, careful to avoid the tips, and I pull with every bit of my might.

I am about thirty thousand bits of might short of what is needed for this job, but I cannot stop. Becky stands poised again with the sticker as I pull. But my goodness, this is a lot of bull. Bulls are shockingly heavy, as it turns out.

And a shocking is what we get. She sticks him again — and I am blown back. The electrical charge shoots through the stick, through the shoulders and the massive neck and even bigger head. It shoots through the horns as if they were wired up for the sole purpose of shocking, and I am jolted to my core.

I am sitting on the ground, shaking my aching head, when I see her approach him one more time.

I go right back and grab those horns.

"You do have trouble learning your lessons, Zane," she says. She does actually look somewhat pained to have to do it again. But she looks equally committed.

A great groan comes out of Highlander.

I look at him and find he's looking at me. Through the curtain of red bangs, I see his big round eyes looking intently at me. And as I pull, and pull, and pull, he makes a huge effort and creates the most remarkable illusion — that I am lifting a beautiful brute bull off the ground by the horns.

"Well," Becky says, "that worked out best for all of us, didn't it?"

He falls in line and starts to walk where Becky wants him to walk. But not before giving me one more long, soft, knowing look.

— · —

I am back in my cell, sitting on the slab as I try to work it out. My clown outfit lies on the bed next to me.

"This is where they actually keep you?" Fuze says, poking her head in. "Your old room is better, I think."

"Stay out of my room, Fuze."

Hugo comes trotting in. "My nose has been places you don't want to know about, but even I think this place smells raunchy."

"Are you okay?" Fuze asks. "You don't look so good."

"I think I'm losing," I say. "I think they're actually defeating me."

"That's good," Hugo says. "The sooner you get defeated, the sooner they'll let you come home."

I give him a look. He wanders out to smell things in other stalls.

"Fuze, did the doctor say anything on the way down here?"

"About you? Oh, my goodness, yes. He's not very pleased with you at this point."

"No, I mean about those collars the animals wear."

"No, but we brought a whole load of new ones down. They are switching them for the old ones right now. Then we have to go."

"Then what, you take them back to the office?"

"No, that giant person in the suit takes them. Back to the Company, is what the doctor kept saying."

Naturally, the Company is involved. The doctor does all kinds of advanced and bizarre work on behalf of the military, and in exchange he is some kind of all-powerful being who can do what he wants to the likes of me *and* become rich and famous and obnoxious at the same time. It's like he's his own country.

There is a big squeal followed by a lot of panicked barking. Hugo comes sailing around the corner, hotly pursued by a big pink blob with teeth. Hugo jumps into my lap, while Pinkish Hugh stands there growling at him. Well, a squealy pig growl.

"Fuze," I say, "meet Pinkish Hugh. Hugh, Fuze."

"My goodness, you are cute," Fuze tells Hugh.

Hugh melts. He lets her hug him. He purrs. Well, a squealy piggish kind of a purr.

"I don't know if this is any help," Fuze says, still embracing the pig, "but do you want to know what it says on the side of the collar?"

"What it *says*?" I jump up to check out Hugh's collar. Hugh snaps at me.

"It's okay, darlin'," she says to him softly, "he's with me."

And just like that, the world's nastiest pink critter calms down.

"What are you, a pig whisperer?" I ask.

"I do have friends in porcine circles," Fuze replies.

I cautiously approach P-Hugh while Fuze soothes him. When I get close enough, I read: THE GRISTLE CATTLELIVID™ CONVERTER.

I back away, staring. I sit on my bunk again where Hugo sits.

"Does that mean anything?" Fuze asks.

"I'm not sure exactly," I say. "But it would appear that these collars are part of the reason the Primeval Ranch has the angriest cattle on earth."

"I'm not cattle," Hugh says to me. "But boy, am I angry."

I nod at him. Then we hear the approach of the mastermind brothers — or, anyway, the mastermind and Bucky.

"Okay, Fuze," I say quickly, "you really want to take over for me, and you really want to help the animals and all?"

"And hang around in your room if I want to?"

"Grrr."

"Hey, you sound just like Hugo."

"Grrr," Hugo says.

"Yes, fine," I tell her. "You can hang around my room."

"Okay, so?"

"You have to get in with Gristle."

"No problem. He's really very nice when you get to —"

"Stop saying that stuff. All I need you to do is, get his confidence, and get him to explain to you what this CattleLivid™ Converter thing is all about so we can figure out what to do about it. Okay?"

The brothers have arrived.

"Oh, a party," Dr. Gristle says.

"A pig party," Bucky says.

Pinkish Hugh pulls away from Fuze, in a panic at the sight of the doctor and his cruel little tool kit. But he's cornered.

They set on him and, before the pig can even struggle, the collar is stripped off him just like stripping the bark off a tree.

Hugh goes wild with pain, and blasts his way through the crowd, out of my cell, out of the stables altogether.

One wicked brother stands there holding a sparkling new CattleLivid™ Converter, while the other stands holding one piggishly soiled and shedding blood droplets and tiny bits of pink pork. The fuss has caused a ruckus in the stalls alongside us in either direction.

"What should we do now?" Bucky asks. "He's naked."

"I'll go get him," Fuze calls. "I'm famous with pigs."

"I'll go with her," I say, and the two of us race with Hugo out into the yard to catch up with Pinkish Hugh while the Gristles go to work changing collars on the other big beasts.

By the time we catch up with him, he isn't even running anymore. He's standing on the narrow road between the paddocks that hold Bistro and the Highlander. But really, you wouldn't even say the pens were holding them, since a fencing of dental floss and tissue paper could hold them now.

"You know," Fuze says, "I don't mean to insult you and your friends here, but is this some kind of wimpy prison ranch, or what? These bulls . . . I mean, it was bad, the bullfighting thing, but shouldn't they be in better shape than this?"

"I don't know," I say. "It's part of what they're doing to them, I guess."

"Hey," says a loud voice right behind us. I jump.

"Edmund!" I gasp. "What are you doing here?"

He's a bit breathless. "I tried to stay away, but I couldn't resist the clown show. Did I miss it?"

"Missed it."

"Aw. I ran. Go put it back on."

"No. Cut it out."

"Hi," Fuze says, tapping Edmund on the shoulder.

"Hi," he says, shaking her hand. "I'm Edmund. I live in a tree."

"That is so cool," Fuze says.

"Don't listen to her," I say. "She thinks everybody's cool."

"Not you," she says.

The pig laughs, and I see the brothers now heading our way.

"Hey, hey," I say, "Pinkish, how would you like to get away before they can slap another one of those things around your neck?"

He is noticeably less combative already.

"Well, duh, stupid."

"Good. Edmund, what do you think? Could you whisk him away and see that he doesn't get found?"

"That's a lot of pig for whisking, Zane."

"Come on, man, they're almost here."

"They?" Edmund says, then turns to see. "Oh, Susanna! It's *them*. Come on, pig man, let's go."

So, pigs can fly. The two of them race up the road fast enough that they are out of reach, if not out of sight.

"Edmund?" Bucky says.

"Is that his name?" I ask. "He just called himself the Wolf, and said if I didn't give up the pig he was going to blow my house down."

"It's true," Fuze says. "Those were his exact words."

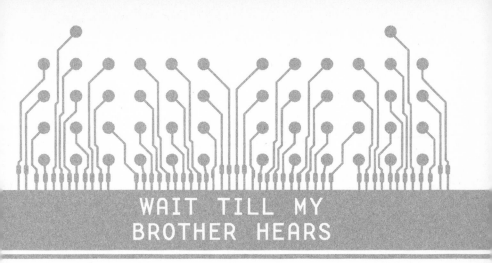

Fuze is delivering on the job of finding the story behind the CattleLivid™ Converter. I can trust her with it because, as much as she can set me off like a rocket, I also know she cares about the animals like I do. She won't stand by and let them suffer if she has anything to say about it.

And she has something to say about everything.

"I heard the details before we even got back," she reports to me later that evening, right after dinnertime. "He was telling it all to his assistant or whatever that thing is in the space suit."

"I call them Gristlies," I tell her.

"Sounds about right," she says.

She's in my room — I know, it's my own fault — and sitting at my computer. I'm in my cell, nursing my many injuries and refueling over a nice tepid platter of hash and beans. Oh, and there is a beet on my plate today, but I think it's just an afterthought since it's still got root and clumps of dirt attached.

"Well," she continues, "he started talking and then looked at me. Said he would discuss it later, because I was there. So I started telling him how much I admired him and thought he could be president because he had a nice smile and all. . . ."

"That's the stuff. He falls for the phony baloney flattery every time."

"What phony baloney? That's all true. Once you are up close, that man has got a lot of charisma. And he was driving. You know, he's a very good driver —"

"Fuze!" I'm rubbing my forehead, trying to massage the nonsense right out before it can take root.

"Okay, anyway, he decided he could trust me when I added what a no-good weenie you were, so I was allowed in when it was time to unload the collars at this building full of whatevers dressed just like that space-whatever we already had with us. . . ."

I hear a commotion out in the yard. All the usual animal milling about is interrupted by the organized chaos that always comes with the bloodhound gang being taken out for a hunt.

"Hurry, Fuze," I say, sensing myself getting pulled into something.

"Okay, well, the place stinks, right? It burns your nostrils open to twice their normal size with the burning, harsh, stenchy stench —"

Dogs coming nearer, Bucky shouting.

"Fuze, please."

"Bio-Battery Acid, Zane."

"Huh?"

"Those ceramic brick things around the animals necks? They're power cells. Like, super power cells. Those wires are part of the madness, making the animal as mental as possible. Then the animal's chemicals and adrenaline and bile and monster hormones and the electrical whatever all gets together and . . . it's like they're milked. Those tubes drip the liquid, the liquid anger, out through the tubes into the power cells like battery acid, and I guess it's like the most powerful power cell anybody ever saw. At that building, they were testing them, attaching them to weapons and vehicles and barbecue grills and . . . the whole place was running on them. And running crazy, I might add."

"Zane!" Bucky says, standing in my cageway. "Get up, boy. You can't laze around on the rack yakkin' all day — we have important work to do! We're goin' huntin'."

A picture comes right into my head — of my head. It's mounted high on the wall of Bucky's dining room, between the badger and the bobcat. I look pretty good, but still. . . .

"Don't I even get a running start?" I ask.

"Don't be foolish," he says impatiently. "You're not even close to earning Level Three discipline yet."

Not yet. I'd better pick up the pace. Undermining any and all hunting sounds like a good place to start.

"That Edmund wasn't here long, but he was nothing but trouble to me while he was here," Bucky says as we ride along behind the pack of dogs. I knew I liked Edmund for a reason. We are headed, unfortunately, in the right direction, up the trail toward the orchard and the Titanium Tree beyond. Bucky is in front of me on a big chestnut racehorsey thing that is as beautiful as he is rude. He could not possibly have to relieve himself as frequently as he is doing here. And if he lifts his tail and farts at me with even a little more heat and force than last time, I will be bald and eyebrow-free before we reach our destination.

My trusty vehicle, Mercury the pony, cannot stop laughing.

The dogs are getting louder and louder, until their yeowling howling joins up into one colossal, irritating soundsplotch.

"So why just not leave him be?" I ask Bucky.

"He ain't getting away with my pig."

"You know," I say, "I have a theory that a pig, or any other animal, can't really belong to a person. And so really, he's his own pig and there's no reason to go after him. We can pick apples or something nice instead."

Bucky pauses in thought before speaking. More likely, he pauses to get control of his temper. "Try not to have theories, Zane. They ain't nothin' but trouble."

And so we ride. Up over the hill, down the short slope through the riverless valley, through the dry and drier until we reach the instantly delicious damp apple air of the orchard.

It's so soothing, the instant one enters.

As long as that one is me.

The dogs, the horses, the Bucky, all seem as intent as before, focused on straightening out our currently pigless situation. They barely even break stride, hovering with their noses an inch from the ground even as they hurtle forward and sideways at full speed.

Pig perfume has to be one of the easier scents to follow, so, really, they're acting a little more triumphant than necessary when we get to the area of the Titanium Tree. They whoop and wild like they just discovered the source of all the world's french fries.

Not that they know what to do with their discovery.

They run around and around the big tree base so hard they might start a whirlpool that swallows everything up. I hop off Mercury, and he takes immediate advantage to go apple shopping. Bucky climbs down off his horse — who, of course, stands there like a good little chestnut security guard.

"What's wrong witcha, boys?" Bucky asks the dogs rather foolishly.

I *am* able to talk to dogs, and I wouldn't be able to get a word out of this lot. I couldn't even tell you if there's a chip in the group, they are so deranged with the job at the tips of their noses.

They are driven crazy by the fact they can't follow a trail now. They aren't hopping up around the base of the tree as if they have cornered something up there. They are running in a great circle because that is all the trail can tell them. The tree has swallowed the pig and the boy, scent and all.

Bucky, the kind of buck who believes whatever a bloodhound says, is stupefied. First he just stares at them running around the tree. Then he paces back and forth right under the gaping cave mouth without even noticing it, six feet up. Then, like with most simple animals caught up in pack mentality, he joins in the run, hopping in line and circling the tree with everyone else.

I step back, take a seat on the ground, and watch the circus go by over and over again.

"Wait till my brother hears about this," Bucky says after about two dozen laps, exhausted, dropping to the ground next to me. "He really, really hates it when we lose an animal that has one of them dang stupid chips in 'em."

"I already heard," says the small voice from my upper arm. I unclip my Gizzard™ and look at Dr. Gristle's toothy, unsmiling miniature fright of a skull face.

"Nice to see you again," I say, not entirely or even remotely truthfully.

He ignores me. "Bucky, just get back to the ranch and

prepare. We are coming back. Right away. I will look into the pig problem when I'm there."

"What are you coming back for?"

Bucky sounds even more tired now, and not much more thrilled than I am at the return visit.

"There is great demand. For the product. I am bringing . . . a friend. So far, my . . . friend is very, very impressed with the . . . product. He wants to see the operation for himself — the process, the system. And we need to really pump up the intensity of the program. This is it, Buck. This could be the big one."

"The big what?" Bucky asks through a clueless Gristle electro-grin.

"The big shut-up-and-go-get-ready, you oaf. You need to *ready* those animals for our special guest tomorrow. *Ready* them into a frenzy."

"Right," Bucky says, his mad smile and dancing orange eyes indicating a frenzy is already under way. He claps his hands and that awful, obedient, autofarter of a horse runs right over to collect him. Bucky whistles, and all the dogs break off from their endless holding pattern around the tree to lead an exhausted and brainless howling charge right back where they came from. "Come on, Zane, get on your horse," he adds.

Which is pretty funny, since at that very moment Mercury does his bit by walking straight up to me and standing on both of my feet. I look like I've got my feet stuck in wet cement, my arms flailing wildly as I try to free myself. Mercury laughs right through until he steps back and watches me tumble straight away and flat onto my back.

I look up and see two faces, one a thirteenish boy and one a Pinkish pig, staring down at me from an unpiggably high opening in the ivy of the world's unlikeliest foliage.

"You do know what you have to do," Fuze says as I sit slumped over my tasty evening meal in my cell. The staff here have spent the afternoon torturing and taunting and infuriating a bunch of noble beasts to the point where they are murderous — all to fuel their power cells. Bucky and Becky have been using their implements of destruction and backbreaking labor to infuriate them. They made Clyde pull a plow, blindfolded, up the biggest hill in the area. They sprayed Bistro with cologne until he now hates himself as well as everyone else . . . *and* he can't stop sneezing. They teased and backcombed Highlander's hair until he deliberately ran himself into a tree.

They tried to get me to do the same, but I simply went on strike. This got me into far hotter water than any bath I'd be taking. Until they realized I enraged the animals my own special way. Just by being there. And trying to convince them I was on their side.

"What?" I say pleadingly to Fuze. "I have to do what? Tell me. I know, I have to remove the CattleLivid™ Converters from all the animals."

"No, dodo, they'll just replace them."

"What, then?"

"You have to make the Converters not work anymore. You have to neutralize them."

I wait, but not for long.

"Yes?"

"You have to make them happy, Zane. The animals. You have to make them happy."

You can sense how dead the whole ranch is right now. Every last animal is drained from the torment of the afternoon, and they're all now unwittingly resting up to be good and strong for the morning, which will only make the program look better. Bucky and Becky, after all that hard work and then sitting down to a modest feast of a bunch of animals wrapped around a bunch of other animals, probably fell asleep in their dessert plates.

When Edmund climbed to the top of Titanium Tree to call and check what was happening here, I summoned him on down. I could hear Pinkish Hugh in the background marveling at the view from the nest. Safe to say, his horizons are broadening and he won't be in a rush to live here again.

"Psst," I hear as I drift in and out of consciousness on my bunk. "Pssst. Pssst."

I hop up, for a second thinking a rattlesnake had infiltrated my cell.

"Hey," says Edmund, his face pressed between the bars.

"Great," I tell him. "Open up."

As a veteran of lockbreaking around here, Edmund wastes all of six seconds on the job, and I'm free. When the door swings open, I see his stout pink pal hard by his side.

"You guys are getting pretty tight," I say.

"He's my bro," Edmund says, surely meaning it.

P-Hugh smiles. Turns out he has dimples.

"Right," Edmund says, clapping his hands together quietly. "Let's go spread the joy."

Though I am not certain what that joy will be, I creep with my associates into the night. We pass by all manner of resting ranch life. Poultry with heads tucked under wings, goats and sheep curled up or sleeping upright. I sense, without quite seeing, owls and bats doing their thing in the air above us. There is a bluey moonlight helping us see, but the nightfliers are onto that.

The big guys, though, are the thing. We walk out to the area where the bulls and horses rest in their pens, their deep breathing and quiet snorting floating on the air like things that are going to be visible if we keep looking.

We stop between paddocks and I turn to the others.

"So then," I say, "how do we go about making the world's angriest beasts happy?"

"I'd say you start by letting them out of captivity," Edmund suggests.

"Isn't that a little dangerous?" I ask.

I ask a bit late because he is already unlatching the gate on Clyde's pen. "It's fine," he assures me. "We'll just open the individual enclosures and keep the main gate closed. That way we'll all be kept in here together."

"I ask again," I say as the towering bulk of a Clydesdale comes walking my way, "isn't that a little dangerous?"

"They'll be great. The whole gathering-together thing will work like a charm. Everybody likes to feel part of a community."

"Um, Ed. You do live by yourself in a hole in the trunk of a tree."

"Now, Zaniac, I hardly live alone. The whole world lives with me."

I'm staring straight up into the massive defined chest of Clyde when Edmund notices and comes over between us. He starts rubbing the great muscles of the horse, patting him hard with both hands and gently bumping his head into him. "It's how you treat 'em," Edmund says. "They respond to respect."

Clyde cranes his neck downward, right over Edmund, to look me in the eye. His eye is big and sparkly. Mine is clouded with fears.

"I respect him," I say. "I respect him so much I may need to change my underwear. Why does he hate me? He hates me and he loves you."

"I keep telling you, Chips Ahoy," P-Hugh says to me,

"the answer is in the chips. Any chipped human is the enemy as far as they know. You have to win them over."

"Rats," I say. "Winning over is one of the hardest winnings of all."

There is a bump at my back. I turn my head to look.

Bistro has bumped me. Now that he sees I have seen, he bumps me again.

"Ah, puke." I feel like I am going to die. Right here, in the dark, because these creatures don't understand me and they are artificially angry. Who could blame them, really? They need somebody to take it out on, and my goodness, these are some unbelievably big muscles on these guys, like they've been getting bigger as they've gotten angrier. And I'm easy to brutalize because I refuse to use the slapstick.

I gently limbo myself down, out of the potential crush of the big guys.

"Take them to the ring," I say to Edmund. "Can you do that?"

He makes a clicking sound with the back of his tongue and they follow like it is a hypnotic suggestion.

"Can I ask what you did with yourself, before you were sentenced to the ranch?" I ask him.

"I grew up on a ranch," he says casually.

I run up to the building at the side of the yard where Bucky stores stuff and Pinkish originally humiliated me by locking me in the weigh crate. I find what I need and run back to the ring, carrying the slapstick high into the crowd of animals.

There is an anxious, uncomfortable stirring. Animals run away, in circles, into each other with great solid thumps. Clyde rears all the way back up on his hind legs and cross-my-heart-filled-throat, he's a hundred and twenty-five feet tall.

"No, no," I say to the disassembled assembled. "You have me all wrong . . . again."

I take the slapstick, raise it high with both hands, and bring it crunching down across my knee.

The crunching sound is, in actuality, my knee.

"Ohhh," I squeal more authentically than Hugh ever dreamed of. "Owww!" I hit the ground and proceed with the writhing and whimpering portion of the program.

I do believe the core of the slapstick may indeed be metal.

I wouldn't call what I'm doing crying, but I don't know if I could honestly call it not crying.

And what do you know, the animals are amused.

P-Hugh's laugh is already fairly familiar, sounding the same in my ear noodle and out in the broader atmosphere. The laughs of the others would be totally foreign to both my ears. But I recognize them all the same. The effect is like a chorus of neighs, of horses sounding like happy horses, and bulls sounding like bulls imitating the sound of happy horses.

And it all sounds fine to me.

I get to my feet, nearly topple over with the horrific pain in my knee, and again the crowd is pleased.

It doesn't last, though.

I am at a loss for my next trick, plus I realize there still is the issue of the slapstick. The way every creature looks at it, it's obvious everyone has a history with the thing.

So I do it again, hold the slapstick over my head with both hands, in a kind of offering to all its victims. They seem to like the gesture, in a vague sort of way.

But no way am I breaking my leg with it, no matter how amusing they find that.

"Um, Zane, now what?" Edmund asks.

"I don't know," I say, feeling stupid enough to please them mightily, but not in quite a visual enough way.

Until . . .

A flash, a six-foot flash of wingspan appears out of the dark, swoops on me, and grabs the slapstick. Shocked, I hang on while the powerful owl accelerates, and my feet are off the ground. It's like I'm hanging on to a trapeze.

I can sense the pleasure of the animals, can feel the goodwill that has been missing, and it cheers me instantly. I feel the thrill in my belly and the rush of mighty wingpower.

"You better let go, or you're gonna die!" Edmund calls.

I see the wisdom of his words as my feet are four feet off the ground and traveling fast.

No need for me to let go, though. The owl has reached the edge of the ring, and my heels neatly clip the top bar of the fencing.

I snap off that trapeze and do a midair somersault so fast that I am facedown in the thick protective sand outside the ring before I can even close my astonished mouth.

My mouth is full of sand. My ears are open, however, and they hear that I am a hit.

Wow. I guess if I lose a limb or kill myself, they will never be angry again.

And much as I love them all, I don't think I can go that far for their entertainment.

I crawl back through the fence rails to a general feeling of agreeability as everyone happily watches the retched slapstick disappear into the night sky. But I am feeling the pain already, banged and bruised, rattled and sleepy this deep into the night, before what will probably be a rocking morning. I just don't know if I am up to making these creatures as happy as they need to be to undermine the vile CattleLivid™ program.

Edmund is doing his bit, the experienced ranch-hand thing, stroking, massaging, whispering to the guys so smoothly you would swear he was their personal counselor. But if this is our pace of progress, the joy will not be spreading like wildfire. Already those waiting for the spa treatment are getting antsy, pawing at the earth and eyeing me like a sparring partner.

"I have to tell you, Edmund, I don't really know what else I can do. What do they like?"

"Clown outfit," Pinkish Hugh says from right behind me. I can actually feel the breath accumulating as the whole rest of the crowd circles in closer.

"Excuse me?"

"The clown outfit. They like you in the clown outfit. There was a noticeable decline in the amount of hate for you when you were dressed like the clown as opposed to . . . whatever it is you are now."

I sigh. It's late. I'm sleepy.

"Oh, go on," Edmund teases. "Make the little ones happy. How committed are you, after all, to winning them over, and rescuing them from that evil program?"

So now I'm an entertainer for children's parties. Gigantic, hairy, heavy-breathing children with lethal horns and hooves.

You know the legend about red rags making bulls wild? That's nothing. You want to make a bull wild? You want to make a bull and all his bull friends and all their horse friends . . . and then rams and alpacas and the whole animal kingdom go wild? Well, here's a hint how.

I am no sooner back in the ring with my colors flying, my wig sparkling in the moonlight, than there is an absolute frenzy. I have to run faster than I ever have to escape an instantaneous mauling at the horns of a number of beasts at once. I am half saved by the mere fact that there is such a crush, such a mad scramble for so many big beasts to bash me at the same time in such a limited space, that they bump one another out of the way, trip, crash fence posts, and even tangle up like collided cartoon racers.

"The barrel!" Edmund calls through his own hysterical laughter.

I make a mad dash for the super-reinforced padded barrel sitting in the corner of the ring and dive just in time to feel a sharpish horn catch the inside underside of my underwear area and not so gently *assist* me headlong into the thing.

I'm safe, anyway.

Until an intercontinental ballistic missile hits me.

Bull-istic is probably more like it.

The first hit sends the barrel toppling end over end over end, and causes uncontrolled celebration out there in the night. This is followed by another and another. There's a kick right there, oh then some clever creature appears to be nosing me like a peanut across the whole playground.

In no time at all, we have what I take to be a full-scale cattle soccer game going on, and all I can do is plead that somebody puts me in the net before we go to sudden death.

I swear, I have never heard an animal celebration like what's going on now. Eventually I become so disoriented from spinning around at about Mach 3 that I go mostly limp. I bang off of every fence post, head, hoof, and finally a nice pop in the air, finished by a thump back to earth that forces my beloved rainbow fright wig to eject itself out into the atmosphere, bringing the gamesbeasts to a final frenzy of delight.

I have no idea how long I am lying there on my side. And I don't care. This is the most comfortable I have felt in a long time. Whoever did the padding in this barrel is a master craftsman.

"I think you were a monster hit," Edmund says, kneeling down next to me.

"This is a quality barrel," I say. "I don't see rodeo clowning as a career choice, though."

"Maybe just a hobby."

"Maybe that, yeah."

"You okay here while I put these guys back where they belong?"

"Wait," I say, making a most feeble pawing attempt to get myself out, "you'll probably need my help. . . ."

He puts a hand on my head, which is far more than enough to subdue me. "You just rest your bones. You've done enough. This is one passive batch of pussycats we have out here at the moment."

"Oh, good," I say, smiling, satisfied. I let my head fall to the side to rest.

I see Edmund lead the animals back to the sleeping quarters, and I see the passive pussycats all over the yard now.

Then, I see nothing. Not nothing, but my multicolor wig, in my face. I reach and pull it back up — only to come face-to-hairy-face with Highlander. He's looking at me with that eye, that look, like when I helped him up after the bullfight. He snorts right in my face, then moves off slowly to bed.

It's the right kind of snort.

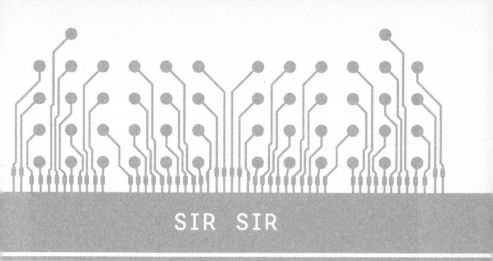

SIR SIR

For the first time, I witness rain at the ranch. When I wake up, it is not merely precipitating, it is bucketing.

"What happened to your uniform?" Becky asks, standing there dripping in my cell. She's holding my clown outfit in her hands, giving it a going-over.

"Uniform? What, am I in the clown army now?"

I don't really even have the energy to sit up and sass her. She'll have to settle for a sidesaddle sass attack.

"There is a tear in this, in the . . . upper posterior thigh area."

"One of your bulls tried to tailor me."

"Well, try not to let this show during the exhibition today."

"I'll keep it tucked in."

"Now here, eat this. It's getting late. They'll be here any second, and they won't be in any mood for dillydally."

For this I sit up.

My breakfast has arrived. All I can tell for certain is

that it is not on a tin plate, and it is actually giving off almost an aroma.

I hop up, nearly topple over again with fatigue and head thrump, but recover rapidly when I realize what I am faced with. It's a large grease-stained brown paper bag, and when I take it and look inside I want to yodel. Because it contains a range of warm and fresh-baked goods: raspberry Danish, hot cross buns, knotted almond-molasses rolls.

I look from the bag, up to Becky. I try to speak, but words don't come. I go back to the bag.

"Bucky says don't you dare leave one bite of that stuff because there will be no sluggishness tolerated. Not from anyone. The whip is cracking today."

And on that note, my angel of mercy and butteriness is gone.

I almost lose fingers in the battle against sluggish-ness, but I bravely soldier through the batch. It is with a spring in my step and a riot of clown color all over that I walk out into the yard, into the hardest rain I ever remem-ber seeing.

I feel the tiny water rockets penetrating even my thick polyester head of hair, a battering of brain pain rain.

The assembly in the ring is a sorry thing indeed. The main stars of the team have been selected — Clyde and Bistro and the Highlander, of course, plus another couple of bulls and horses. Dr. Gristle is standing in his white

Dr. Insanity outfit, just in case nobody knows who he is. Behind him are two of his faceless space goons, and next to him, arms folded across a large chest full of medals and ribbons and letters and numbers and faces and Chinese characters and advertisements for rocket fuel additives and sports drinks that are made from the same main ingredient, is the guest of honor.

"Don't be staring at Sir Sir," Bucky commands when I stop still in wonder.

"My clown outfit is funeral gear next to that," I say, chuckling.

"We'll all be in funeral gear if you get us on the wrong side of that guy," Bucky says, "so just make like you don't even know he's there. Your job is to work with me and Becky here in the ring and get these animals just as worked up and worked out as possible, so Sir Sir can see what it is we do here on this project."

"What exactly do we do?"

He looks at me with a puzzled, openmouthed face. Then he screws it into a scowl. "Very important stuff, that's what," he says, pulling me into the ring. "So let's go."

I can't help stealing glances at Sir Sir. Dr. Gristle is one of the tallest people I've ever seen, but this guy looks to be another six inches into space beyond that. His glasses things might be adding a couple of inches, because he is in this smoked-glass wraparound, up and over setup that is almost a combination of glasses and the top one-quarter of a helmet.

The rain hits the hel-glass like bullets, sparking away again in all directions. It adds to the rain hitting Dr. Gristle nearby — his own fault for being cool and uncovered.

My colleagues in this show are standing there soaking up rainwater and looking glum, but I know better. I see now, in their eyes, there is something greater than that now inside them. I see it because the animals are the animals and I am the Friend. And now that they let me, I know I can help them — and they know it, too.

Community, like Edmund said.

"Go get 'em, clown-boy," Edmund's voice says in my ear. He's up in the nest, in this monsoon. In a metal tree, fishing for lightning.

"Send me a postcard when you reach the next galaxy," I say.

Bucky and Becky approach us slowly yet firmly, and I feel just like a member of the herd.

I love that feeling.

The rain seems to make things go faster, with more urgency. Bucky lacks even his usual minor subtlety.

"Move!" he shouts as he jabs at Clyde with his electronic devil fork. Clyde starts moving, and one by one each bull, each horse, each clown gets into the train that chugs around the perimeter of the ring like something between a criminal lineup and a circus march.

Either way, humiliating.

"Don't worry about it, guys," I say, patting the mountainous rump in front of me. "It will all be over soon. You're all champions, every one of you."

The rain manages to get even harder.

"Hey, Zane," Edmund says, and I whip around to see him because he's right there.

Only he's not.

"I think the storm makes this doohickey work even better. I can hear so clearly now. I can hear your heartbeat, man. Did you drink a trough full of coffee, by the way?"

"Stage fright," I say.

Dr. Gristle bellows something at Bucky. I look over to see Sir Sir still standing there with his arms folded, looking like something constructed, inorganic. Gristle is the opposite, flailing, shouting, pointing.

Bucky responds by climbing on the back of a smallish palomino horse and digging him so hard with spurs he draws blood instantly. He rides him around and around, like a loon who has never learned to ride, who has never even seen a horse that moves its own legs rather than just going up and down and around and around on a pole. Bucky kicks him and yanks at him and shouts at him and slaps. All the animals, in turn, get agitated.

"Bring him over," Dr. Gristle says after this goes on for five excruciating minutes.

Bucky rides the palomino right over to the fence, where the doctor rushes up and snaps a small handheld meter onto a spot on the CattleLivid™ Converter.

"That is hardly enough," Gristle growls at his brother. He is speaking in that deranged angry voice, where he tries to whisper, but people can feel the vibrations through the ground for about two miles.

"This ain't good," Edmund reports from air traffic control.

"Nope," I say.

It's not even orderly now, the way all the animals are running about. No more simple parade route as Bucky rides wildly back into the middle of things and stirs everybody in different directions. Becky goes around randomly stabbing any haunches that run past.

I hop onto the smallest animal in the vicinity.

"You guys are creeps," Mercury says in a pained and desperate voice.

"They are. I'm not," I say, clinging to his neck. I can feel the snaps of electricity running through me as I make contact with his Converter. "Just hold on," I say. "Hold on, and this will pass."

I feel another surge, a fraction of what he must be feeling.

"No," he says, "Why don't *you* just hold on."

And he jams on his brakes.

As Mercury bends his neck low, I fly hawkspeed right over him and six feet beyond before landing, several times, with a crash into the muddy earth.

There is a pause all around. Everyone concerned with my well-being, naturally.

I don't know what this sound sounds like to the rest of the humanoids. But when I raise my mud-caked, frizzy, rainbow-topped head from the ground, the sound in my head is the greatest symphony of laughing voices in human and nonhuman history.

You know, how awesome is the laugh that you really, really need?

"You surely need to turn professional," Edmund cackles into my ear.

I stand, and bow, and wave, and look to the stands. . . .

Sir Sir shows no sign of recognition. Or life.

His pal Gristle, on the other hand, dashes right through the fence rails and into the field of play. He rushes up to one animal after another, slapping the meter on each one. He shakes his mad, soaked white head. "No, no, not good enough — not, not at all."

He looks like he's about to burst. "Right," he says. "Right. Bucky, Becky — we're running out of time. Stop wasting our time. That man, Sir Sir, is the single busiest man on earth. He is responsible for all the important things that nobody knows about. We have no more time to waste. Get rid of all these wastrel beasts. All of them. Just shoo or rustle, or getalongdoggie, or whatever it is you hick people do. Get their rancid useless carcasses out of this pen now and leave me that one and that one and that one. Do it. Now!"

The gate is open, and Bucky and Becky get all the animals along except for the nominated champions, Clyde, Bistro, and the Highlander. The three of them are pulled together, and Dr. Gristle hauls over a long white contraption, two shiny white extended versions of those ceramic bricks around the Converter collars. He gets Bucky to help him, and together they clamp the three mighty magnificents together, one white strip under their chins, the other behind their heads. They are all plugged in together, into the three CattleLivid™ Converters.

"Sir Sir," Dr. Gristle hollers out, into the rain, with hailstones now bouncing off the immensity of his forehead, as yellow bursts of lightning zap across the sky. "I want to present you now with the technological wonder that uses the past to solve all the problems of the future!"

"Way to undersell there, Doc," Edmund says.

"The modern-day version of the blessed yoke, that will harness brute, ignorant beast power to fuel the genius of my ... er, modern man's greatest global and interglobal ambitions. I present to you, Sir Sir, the Gristle GridLock™!"

It's possible somebody accidentally unplugged Sir Sir's cord from the socket. Because, really, there's no reaction.

Which only makes the Gristles go harder.

The doctor screams and rants demented negative encouragement, while Becky and Bucky get behind and flatly brutalize three of earth's finest beasts. The devils are stabbing, stabbing at them with such force it looks like the conclusion to a hunt about two hundred thousand years ago.

This is, I can see, a whole different ball game. I can actually see sparks coming off the creatures' backs, the rain and elements getting in and under with the wires. The electronic devil forks are doing their work, and the GridLock™ and CattleLivid™ Converters are doing their work, and Pure Prime Evil Human awfulness is doing its work, to finally push these guys over whatever ledge is still out there.

"Do something!" Edmund screams.

I am around in front of the team now, and can see them out of their minds. Eyes so red they are practically showering blood over me.

"Hang in there, guys," I say. "Outlast them. Time will run out on this. You *can* win!"

I don't even know if they can hear me now. They are fairly screaming with rage.

Dr. Gristle keeps running up, tapping the GridLock™ with his meter.

"Getting there," he shouts to Sir Stiffo. "Getting there!"

"Zane!" Edmund shouts. "The barrel!"

"A little late for the barrel."

"Not if someone else gets in!"

Edmund, you genius.

I leave the front of the animals, where I simply can't take their hurting eyes and frothing mouths anymore, and I run around to the rear.

Becky and Bucky are practically on their knees, totally drained with the general frenzy of things and the monstrous effort of turning these rumps to burger.

And this, I realize, is why nature makes some creatures stupider than the others.

"Here," I say to Bucky, "I'll take over for a spell."

"Good boy," he says, handing me his electronic devil fork. He leans over huffing, his hands on his knees.

I walk right up to him, the electronic tines inches from his nose. "Into the barrel, clown," I say.

He looks up, even more dumbfounded than usual. His open mouth collects hailstones like nuts for the winter.

He starts walking, and I am confronted by Becky just as he's climbing in.

"I think not," I tell her, raising my fork over the now barreled hubby. "Drop it, or the Buckster gets it."

See, the smart part was going after him, because as a Gristle, he'd have let her get it.

She drops it.

"Now go up there and make me a real meal," I say, gesturing toward the house. "A pizza."

She runs. I turn to find that doctor demento has actually clambered aboard the smallest of the three and is flailing away at Highlander.

"Hey," I shout, whistle, whoop in as cowboy a way as I can muster.

The team has veered our way, and I can see that they're watching me now.

"Poke your head out," I say to Bucky.

"No," he says, deep in cowering cocoon mode.

"Poke your head out or I'll reach in there and skewer it like a cocktail meatball."

I am not too big a person to confess that I am loving this talk.

The meatball pops up by itself.

And I feel the balance of the universe shift.

Or maybe it is just the weight and might of the team thundering this way that is making the planet shift right off its axis.

I barely make it out of harm's way. First to hit the barrel is Bistro, knocking it into the fence post so hard the rebound comes right back to Highlander, who scores spectacularly on the rebound. The team, working like a true team, swings around to give an absolutely delirious Clydesdale a clear whiplash of a backward kick at the barrel. And another and another.

Another kind of brother would put a stop to this.

It goes on for ages, and it hardly seems to be storming anymore because a different kind of sunshine is now bathing the whole place. Somehow Dr. Gristle sees this as a positive thing because he keeps urging them on, thinking they are so enraged they are going to generate enough power for Sir Sir to wipe three of his favorite baddie countries off the map before naptime.

But the animals are in playland.

"No!" Gristle keeps shouting, into the meter, into the sky. "How can this be? How can the power be going *down*?"

He smacks the gizmo on Highlander's back over and over again in frustration. He stands up and stamps on his back, like the world's most dangerously unhinged infant.

Until nature calls time.

With a crack like the world being born, a shock of lightning comes out of the sky and has a choice to make between Edmund in the Titanium Tree, and our hero here.

Well, what would you do if you were nature?

BUZZZZZZZ

Here's a good thing you can say for Dr. Gristle. There aren't many of them, so I suppose it is fair to say one when you can.

Of all the experiments, all the insane ideas, the gizmos, the gadgets, the silicon and whatever chips, the wires and implants and potions he devises to alter the world as we know it, he is always willing to put his money where his mouth is. Everything he shoots into other creatures is also floating around in his irradiated self.

Integrity or insanity? It's a tough call, but either way he gives off an audible buzz.

And he apparently attracts lightning like a six-foot-six walking golf club.

By the time he wakes up, there on his back in the mud in the middle of the ring in the relaxing rain, calm has been restored.

But he'll put a stop to that.

"It was working!" Dr. Gristle says, leaping unwisely to

his feet. He staggers, starts running completely sideways like a land crab with only two legs, and finally comes to rest with a thump against the fence.

His brother staggers over to his side. Bucky, at about half his original modest height because of his new back problem, isn't a lot of help.

I stand on the opposite side of the ring with my giant pals, unhooked, unleashed, unburdened. And sharing a pizza.

"Would you like to know what I think?" says the newly, barely animated Sir Sir from the other side of the fence.

"Very much," Dr. Gristle whimpers. "Very, very much." He almost topples again, but digs his elbow into his hunchback brother and leans on him in a casual, businesslike fashion.

"I think you should strap that thing to yourself. The amount of lunatic energy you could harness would power your own entire little planet, wherever that unfortunate place might be."

"But this program . . . it's genius. It has the potential to provide the world with all the power it so badly needs, infinitely!"

"And by world, you mean yourself, yes?"

"Yes!" Gristle shouts excitedly. Then he gently covers his mouth with his hand as if he burped instead of revealing his sinister plan for dictatorship of all creation.

"This program is an absurdity," Sir Sir says, "just like its creator."

"You don't understand, Sir Sir, sir. This was sabotage. It was him!"

He points across the way to innocent, minor me, prisoner number 0000002.

"It was him," the Sir says with brilliant obvious disgust. "The child in the clown outfit? Has sabotaged your grand almighty scheme?"

"Yes, I'm telling you. It was him. It's *always* him!"

"He struck you with lightning?"

Gristle takes a deep breath, searches the vastness of his insanity for an explanation, then responds, "Yes! Probably! I'm fairly certain!"

"I see," says Sir Sir from under his little smoked-glass dome. "Dr. Gristle, your mental impairment does not excuse the fact that you have wasted my very important time with this folly. I may not yet control the elements like that little boy over there but trust me, I control just about everything else. If you *ever again* dare to . . ."

The doctor is, in his way, indestructible.

"I'm working on another idea," he says to the departing Sir Sir.

Sir Sir stops, rotates without appearing to use foot-power, and says, "So am I. Are you sure you would like to exchange ideas right now, Doctor?"

The silence that sweeps over is like the arrival of spring.

As Sir Sir and his people-things disappear, Edmund in the tower is overcome with happy thoughts.

"That was the buttwhuppin' of the century," he says ecstatically. "Ain't no Gristles gonna mess with you ever again, Zane."

The doctor and his hunchman have staggered toward us now with a grim sense of purpose. Dr. Gristle is looking up and away.

"Who said that to you?" he demands of me.

Uh-oh.

"Uh-oh," Edmund says.

The lightning. It's charged up all the gear inside him. . . .

"There. There it is again. Who is that? Where is it coming from? How is it happening?"

I am quick on my big clown feet.

"Nothing but the breeze, Doctor."

"What breeze? It said *Zane*. It called you *Zane*."

Even quicker.

"Well, I'm getting kind of well known, Dr. Gristle. When you are as renowned for stuff as I am, your name tends to carry on the wind."

I get a warm encouraging head bump from someone giant and hairy behind me.

"It's coming from up there," Gristle says, looking right

at the spot where he can't see Edmund looking right back. "Bucky, what is that tree there?"

"Big tree," Bucky says, shrugging his shoulder horizontally forward. "Nothing special."

"I'll be the judge of that. Take me there, right now."

All animals everywhere sigh at once.

"Maybe you should take a little break," I call to the two sad crumpled wicked freaks propping each other up along the road.

"Maybe you should start to worry that your game is finally up, young Zane," he calls back.

"He never learns, does he?" Edmund says in my ear.

"No," I say. "It's one of his most lovable qualities. You gonna be okay up there?"

"You kidding?" I can actually hear his ear-to-ear grin. "I learned from the best. I'm gonna be Zane 2.0."

"Oh, the doctor will like that. Bucky, too."

"Bring it *on*," Edmund says.

My work here is done.

"Stay out of my room, Fuze."

"Zane!" Hugo struggles his way out of Fuze's death cuddle and bounds right up into my arms as I step into my room. All the electronic gear, monitors and speakers and lights, camera, action of my home life burst into operation with my return. My parents' big talking heads appear, and they can just talk to each other for a while.

"This is most unusual," I say to Hugo as we hug.

He does not like it when I point out his tender and loving side. He struggles away from my embrace.

"I was confused," he says, "because you smell like butt, ranch-face."

"I missed you, too," I say, laughing.

"The room never acted like this for me," Fuze says, marveling at all the electronic life around us.

"That's because it's not *your room*."

"All right, all right," she says. "I'm going."

She walks past me, and she may be muttering, but I am busy reclaiming my life and my stuff.

"Hey, jerko," Hugo scolds. "That lassie didn't do half bad taking care of things while you were gone. I really like her. If it wasn't for the excessive cuddling I'd seriously consider giving her your job permanently."

"Fuze," I call after she has left the room. She is still standing right outside the door.

"Lorilai," she says.

I do a little growl at her. Hugo does a little growl at me.

"Sorry . . . Lorilai," I say. "Thanks. You did a great job."

"And now you'll stop telling me to stay out of your room."

"Well, um . . . no. But Hugo really likes you."

She laughs and heads down the hall. "I know," she says. "He told me."

I whip around to my dog as the front door slams. "Huh . . . ?"

"What can I tell you," he says, jumping unauthorized onto my bed, "she's a dog person."

I saunter over to him — and suddenly back here in civilization I am aware that I do, in fact, saunter now.

"What is that?" Hugo asks through cackling laughter.

"That, my boy, is the new and manly walk of a rough-and-tumble outdoors hero, conqueror of gnarly beasts, defeater of evil vets and people who wear spurs, champion and supreme Friend of animals everywhere. It's my saunter, kiddo."

You'd think that would put an end to the cackling.

You'd think.

"Well, Friend, your legend has indeed spread among animals far and wide, and I am proud to be your roommate, but that walk looks like a bad case of heat rash."

I plunk down on my bed, grab his great noggin in a headlock.

"Speaking of rash, Hugo, you looked awfully cute in that diaper. I bet Fuze left a few. . . ."

"Saunter, Friend. I'll call it saunter, and we'll call it even."

"Even," I say, releasing his head and shaking his paw.

"Oooh, strong grip, too," he says.

"Don't push it, Hugo."

"Sorry. It really is heat rash, though, isn't it?"

"Maybe a little."

End of Book Three